GROVER

To Marian—
Because—

Vera A. Cleaver

Bill Cleaver

Lutz, Florida
March. '70

GROVER

VERA and BILL CLEAVER

Illustrated by Frederic Marvin

J. B. LIPPINCOTT COMPANY
Philadelphia and New York

TO

Mell Busbin

WITH

ESTEEM

AND

MORE

GROVER

Chapter One

In Grover's opinion cows were the dumbest animals alive. They figured their stomachs were strong enough to digest almost anything they felt like putting in them but then, when they found out differently and got sick, all they did was lie around and gripe and holler for somebody to come and help them.

This one cow he knew was crazy about cardboard boxes and the people who owned her had a lot of forgetful children so she had become a regular patient of his uncle's. Besides the complications caused from her appetite for cardboard boxes she had a lot of other ailments, too. She liked attention. When she saw Grover and his uncle coming she flopped down in her stall and moaned and groaned like she was dying.

"I can hardly work up any more pity for this old girl," Grover said to his Uncle Ab. "I think her trouble is she just plain doesn't have any sense. What you reckon ails her this time? More cardboard boxes?"

Uncle Ab applied his stethoscope. Sickly placid, the cow turned her head and looked at him. Uncle Ab patted her flank and said, "There, there now. You're going to be all right. Just give me a minute to figure out what's wrong here."

Grover moved around to her other side and applied his stethoscope. "Nothing wrong with her heart. It's pumping strong. If you want my opinion I think this old girl is a hypochondriac. I think she enjoys being sick."

The cow rolled her head back in Grover's direction, blinked her sad eyes, and let out a big, hot belch. It smelled like glue.

Uncle Ab returned his stethoscope to his bag and sat back on his haunches. The cow burped a couple of times and weakly flicked her tail.

Grover returned his stethoscope to his bag and sat back and waited for the diagnosis.

"I don't think it's anything serious," said Uncle Ab with professional calm. "Let's just wait a few minutes and see what happens."

Grover said, "If I had my way I'd give her a quart of castor oil and turn her loose and see how she liked that. Dumb cow. I swear I don't see where you get your patience with these animals, Uncle Ab. Sometimes they aggravate the heck out of me. Sometimes I don't know whether I want to become a veterinarian or not."

The cow rolled her glassy eyes, turned a yearning look on Uncle Ab, her stomach rumbled, she tottered to her feet, spent a moment looking uncertain, opened her mouth, her stomach rumbled again and out spewed three or four pieces of undigested cardboard. In disbelief she looked at them, shook her head to clear it and with a relieved look swayed out of her stall. On her way to clean, outside air and sunshine she picked up a big mouthful of hay.

Grover said, "See what I mean? She doesn't care that we had to get out of bed to come out here. She didn't need us to sit around here and wait for her to vomit. But no. She had to have an audience like she always does. Dumb, selfish cow."

Uncle Ab laughed.

Sometimes, reflected Grover, being a veterinarian's assistant was kind of disgusting. The work had a lot of drawbacks to it. One of them was that no matter what day it was or what time, when the call came to go, you went.

Driving back to town through the Sunday stillness, Uncle Ab said, "Sunday. When I was a kid I used to hate Sundays so bad I couldn't enjoy Saturdays. Your dad wasn't any too fond of them either. Every week along about Wednesday he'd start working on ways for us to get out of Sunday. One time we mixed up a bar of yellow laundry soap with a plug of good, strong tobacco and on Saturday night we smeared our armpits with it and went to bed that way, but we didn't get the fevers we hoped for. All we got was blisters and a licking. That was back in the good old woodshed days," he added.

Thick with green gloom, the backwoods hammocks through which they traveled smelled dankly of red mangrove. In a stand of high canal grass a coon scrubbed his bandit face with his paws. The road before them was smooth and white and hot. Uncle Ab whistled. Grover glanced at the dashboard clock. It was ten minutes before ten o'clock.

Under the heat of the morning they came into Thicket and parked in front of Lottie's Cafe. The Sunday quiet was heavy, broken only by the mournful tolling of the bell atop the Methodist church. Save for Sheriff Irby Fudge's car parked in front of his office, Main Street was clean and empty and so was Lottie's Cafe save for Lottie.

Lottie always served plenty of conversation along with her food. She said that Farrell, her grandson, was coming to visit her again. She said that she hoped he and Grover could forget their differences and be friends the way they had been during his first summer visit two years prior. That Farrell was nine years old now and had lost his passion for shooting out people's windows with BB guns and blaming it on other people. She said that since Grover was two years older than Farrell she thought he should be the one to apologize first for all of their past fights. When Grover said he'd consider it she gave him two extra pats of butter for his buckwheat cakes.

Sheriff Fudge came in and announced the temperature. Uncle Ab invited him to sit down and he did and they started a cheerful conversation about politics. During a lull in it Grover said he thought he'd go down to the river and see about his boat and Uncle Ab gave his permission. He had Lottie fix a cold chicken sandwich to take along.

The bell in the tower of the Methodist church had stopped ringing. From end to end Main Street was as silent and motionless as a dead corpuscle. Only the heat waves, lying in dizzying layers, moved.

For as long as his memory went back this town had always been the same: long, drowsy streets roofed over by great shade trees, heat-soaked paths on the outer skirts instead of sidewalks, the fields lying between it,

and the river sucked dry of color and energy. Blind-
folded Grover could find his way through this stretch of
land.

He huffed past a clump of dust-coated bushes and an
old mud-colored bird reared up and glared at him. A
lubber grasshopper wearing the henna-tinted coat of
his maturity, clung to a stalk, devouring it.

On the dark, moist bank of the river a toad floun-
dered. Moored to a tree with a length of rope Grover's
boat gently bobbed in the soup-warm water. His friend,
Ellen Grae Derryberry, was sitting in it chewing gum
and reading a book. She watched him take off his shoes
and slide down the bank and climb in. "Hey, Grover,
you're late," she said.

"No I'm not. I'm early. Church just started. I've been
out to the country with Uncle Ab. Farrell's coming
tomorrow, Ellen Grae. We stopped in at Lottie's for
breakfast and she told me that. I almost promised her I
wouldn't fight with him any more. He's nine now and
that's two years younger than me and one year younger
than you so I just about had to. What are you reading?"

"A book."

"What's it about? No, wait a minute. I don't want to
know. I just want to sit here and let my mind be blank
for a few minutes. Ellen Grae, you remember the bomb
Farrell made two years ago when he was here?"

"No, Grover. How could I remember a thing like
that? Almost every day somebody tries to blow my
head off with a homemade bomb. There's no reason for
me to remember it. It's nothing. Let me read you some
of this book to take your mind off things. It's about

love, I think. A man and a woman in love. Isn't that disgusting? Her name's Jessica and his is Phillip."

"Jessica and Phillip. Already I don't like it. But what are they doing?"

"They aren't doing anything, Grover. They're in love. Wait a minute; let me see if anything happens on the next page. Oh, yes, they . . . no, they're still in love. She's got . . . well, I swear."

"What's the matter?"

"She's got long hair the color of honey and he's winding it around her neck like a noose, choking her with it. And she's just sitting there letting him do it."

"She's just sitting where?"

"In a railroad station in Austria. She's a ballerina and he's a musician and they don't have any money. That's why he's choking her. He doesn't want to. He doesn't want her to starve, that's why. No, wait a minute. That's not the real reason. She's got a husband by the name of Bern and he's coming on the stroke of midnight to take her away. That's the real reason. Phillip's heart is breaking. As soon as he gets through choking Jessica he's going to run and throw himself under a train. That way maybe they'll get together again. You see what I mean? They hope for a better hereafter. Phillip—"

"Phillip makes me sick," Grover said. "And so does Jessica. They sound like a couple of loons to me. I don't know why you waste your time reading books like that, Ellen Grae."

Ellen Grae closed the book and laid it on the cross seat. She tucked her gum in a corner of her cheek and sighed. "I chose it by mistake. I didn't know it was about love. So Farrell's coming, huh?"

"Yeah."

"Too bad," said Ellen Grae, her reaction not surprising him.

Ellen Grae wasn't like most girls. When they went fishing she did her share of the rowing, baited her own hooks, rescued herself when she fell overboard. She hated dresses and shoes and never bawled. She called her parents Jeff and Grace. They were divorced, so most of the time she lived with the McGruders but Grover never had heard her gripe about it. The only thing that aggravated him about Ellen Grae was the way she yakked when he was trying to catch a fish. That morning she had brought him four fat grasshoppers to use for bait but due to her yakking he only landed one little scrawny bass.

Lolling in the stern of the boat she said, "Jeff's gone to Arizona, Grover."

"To paint some more pictures?"

"Yes. He's going to live with a family of Hopi Indians for two weeks on the Painted Desert. You've heard about their beautiful sand paintings? Well, that's what he's gone out there to observe."

"That's nice."

"This family he's going to live with has twenty-nine children. Sometimes don't you wish you had some sisters and brothers, Grover? I do. What are you staring at?"

"That lily pad out there. There's a big fish under it. In a minute he's going to spot my grasshopper and climb out after it. Watch."

Ellen Grae stood up, recinched the belt to her pants, glanced at the lily pad, sat down again, looked at her dirty feet, inched forward and flopped both of her legs over the side of the boat. "The Painted Desert is just beautiful. It looks like somebody's birthday cake. You've seen it, haven't you, Grover?"

"No. Don't rock the boat, Ellen Grae. I'm trying to catch a fish."

"I spent a whole summer on it one time and lived with this big family. The reason I was sent out there was because the doctors thought I had a spot on one of my lungs; they thought I was consumptive. Did I ever tell you about that, Grover?"

"No, Ellen Grae, you never told me about any spot on your lungs and I wish you wouldn't now because I'm trying to catch a fish."

Ellen Grae pulled a long thread from the tail of her shirt and made a bracelet for one of her ankles with it. "It wasn't really a spot. It was my locket which the X-ray technician forgot to ask me to take off when Grace took me for my yearly checkup so you don't have to be afraid of catching anything from me. But anyway, *before* they realized their mistake they sent me out to a sanitarium in Arizona and I stayed with this big family on their ranch. From the attic where I was forced to sleep because there wasn't any room for me anywhere else, I could look out and see the Painted Desert. It really *does* look painted. All red and yellow and white and lavender. It's just lovely. But Arizona is cruel. One time when we were having a roundup I came across a poor man who hadn't had a drink of water for seven days and seven nights. He was dying. Are you listening to me, Grover?"

"Sure, sure. But I don't need to. If I was suddenly to be struck stone deaf I could tell you what happened.

Don't rock the boat, Ellen Grae. I'm trying to catch a fish."

With her tongue Ellen Grae made a pale button out of her gum, sucked it back into her mouth. "It was just terrible," she said. "Coming up on him the way I did. At first I thought he was a dead Gila monster but then, when I wheeled my horse around and took another look at him I realized that he was a man. He was dying. He hadn't had a drink of water for—"

"—seven days and seven nights," Grover said. "He was all dried up; nothing but a sack of old skin and bones. Probably one of his legs was broken or maybe one of his eyes was gouged out. But he was still breathing. When you roared up on your horse and saw him lying there you could tell that. So you jumped down and whipped out your water canteen, only it was empty. But that didn't stop you from saving this poor old wretch. About five feet from where he was lying there was a big cactus, wasn't there?"

"Yes," agreed Ellen Grae with a glassy look. "But listen, Grover, I'm the one who's telling this. You're not supposed to—"

"And you spied it and said to yourself, 'Aha, there's water in that cactus.' And you whipped out your bush knife and ran over to it and whacked its head off and got about a gallon of water out of it and then ran back to this poor old victim and after he got all nice and revived again you carted him off to town to the doctor. Only the doctor wasn't there. Nobody was there. Nobody was because this was a ghost town. But you found an old, abandoned hospital and dragged this old victim into it and got him up on the operating table and gave

him a couple of shots to quiet him down and a couple of
quarts of glucose to get his juices going again and then
you set his leg or whatever it was that was broken and
then—"

"It was his ribs," said Ellen Grae in a faraway voice.
"Four of them were crushed."

"Yeah. It's not clear to me how they got that way
but—"

"His horse fell on him," supplied Ellen Grae and
raised both hands to her eyes, covered them, spread the
fingers and looked at Grover. Her smile was lustrous.

A black catfish with a bristle of whiskers and a mean-
looking bullet-shaped head craftily slid up to the lily
pad and snatched the dead grasshopper from it.

Above a cluster of turkey oaks on the riverbank a
black bird hung balanced. Undisturbed by the heat, the
river, languorously rolling along in its dark corridor,
smelled cool and sweet.

The color of Ellen Grae's straight, skinny legs made
him think of roast beef. He took the forgotten chicken
sandwich from his pocket but they couldn't eat it; it
was soggy with mayonnaise and squashed besides.

So they went home. Ellen Grae to the McGruders
and he to the pastel house on Fox Trot Street. His father was at the phone in the kitchen. His mother sat on
a chair near the door. Her hair hadn't been brushed;
she was still in her nightclothes.

He said, "What's the matter? You sick?"

Her bleached smile had something in it that didn't
belong. "A little. You'd better get washed, Grover."

"What for? It's too late for church. Uncle Ab and I
didn't get back from the country in time. We had pan-

cakes at Lottie's. Hey, lookit this roast; it's still raw. Aren't we gonna eat today?"

There were the funniest tears in his mother's eyes. They were the largest tears he had ever seen but they didn't tremble the way most tears do. They didn't spill over. Behind them her pupils were enormous. She brought her hands up and crossed them, back to palm, and laid them against her mouth. In a tone of strange and unreal sweetness she said, "Oh, Grover," and then the tears spilled over and ran down her face.

Finished with the phone his father put it back in its cradle. He turned and spoke. "Your mother is sick, Grover. She has to go to the hospital. How about giving us a hand with things?"

He looked at the roast, thawing on a square of foil on the drainboard. Now it didn't seem important whether it got cooked or not. Inside him a heaviness had begun to form. There was something secret and stealthy in the air. They were keeping something from him. But he said, "Sure. What things?"

With a sudden, odd eagerness his father walked toward him and placed himself so that Grover couldn't see his mother struggling to get hold of herself. His father placed his hand on the crest of his shoulder and explained to him what had to be done. His mother needed a little surgery but there wasn't a doctor in Thicket who could do it so she would be admitted to the big hospital over in Tampa that afternoon. His father would drive her there and then take a room for himself in a nearby motel for a day or two. Grover would go and stay with Uncle Ab and Aunt Marty. His cooperation was needed. A lot of conversation wasn't.

Go wash. Then get a suitcase from the hall closet and pack several changes of clothing in it. Don't take anything that isn't clean. Don't forget pajamas and toothbrush.

The hall closet was dark and smelled strongly of camphor. He had to use a flashlight and stand on a chair to get the suitcase. It had a lot of stuff piled on top of it and he knocked some of it down while he was trying to get it out; his father, hurrying past, paused to say, "For gosh sake, Grover, you're only going four blocks. Just get the suitcase. If you need anything else in here you can come back for it tomorrow. Your Aunt Marty will have a key to the house."

The heaviness in him had increased. He looked down at his father and in that same instant his father looked up at him and their eyes met. His father's had pain in them and fear and a dreadful anxiety. They looked as if they had been scalded in these three things.

The heaviness in him surged. He said, "Dad?"

His father coughed against his fist. "Not now, Grover. Not now. Just get the suitcase. Just this once do as you've been told without a lot of questions."

He is a good man, my father, thought Grover but were anybody to ask me if I wanted to be like him I would have to say no because with everything and everybody except my mother he is sketchy. He doesn't look at things or listen. It strains him to talk to people.

At one o'clock that afternoon he and his father stood in Uncle Ab's portico and said a temporary good-bye. Chewing his lips, his father said, "I want you to behave yourself now."

Grover said, "I will."

In the car his mother raised her gloved hand and smiled.

His father handed Aunt Marty the key to their house, walked around to his side of the car and got in.

He watched them drive away.

Chapter Two

There was something wrong but it was a secret. He wasn't old enough to be told about it.

They treated him like he was a little kid again; like suddenly he was back in blue rompers, staggering around licking lollipops.

He asked his anxious questions but the smooth answers cheated him. The half-truths in them had good intentions but they didn't help the anxiety and they left him with a still anger. They didn't help the fear that hung in his mind.

Aunt Marty and Uncle Ab whispered of their own fear and worry, in the kitchen and dim hallways, but he was shielded.

Suddenly he was somebody who had to be watched all the time. He was not allowed to stay in his room by himself unless he was asleep. They kept him busy, kept him moving, kept him interested: in what was in the sky, the ground, the garage, and Uncle Ab's office, what was on the book shelves and the radio, today's weather and tomorrow's and food.

He acquired a new power over people, a new influence. He was witty all of a sudden. Everybody laughed at his weak jokes.

All of his big faults fled. Only the little ones were left and they didn't matter.

Talk rattled:

"How is your little friend, Grover? What's her name? Ellen Grae?"

"Yes'm. Ellen Grae. She's fine. Her father's gone to Arizona to study sand painting. Farrell's coming day after tomorrow."

"Farrell? Who's Farrell?"

"Farrell. You know. Lottie's Cafe. Her grandson. Farrell."

"Oh, yes. The little boy who made the bomb."

"Yes'm. That's the one."

Have some more pie. No? Well, maybe after a while. Here, I'll save you this big piece.

No, I don't need any help with the dishes. I'll just let them air-dry here in the rack. Come on, let's take a little cooling ride. Isn't it beautiful out tonight? The stars so clear and close?

Ah, that was a nice ride. Wasn't that a nice ride, Grover? I just love to get out and ride around on Sunday evenings. Thicket's such a pretty little town.

My, the lawn is dry. Everything is. I wish it would rain. Tomorrow I think I'm going to move this row of hydrangeas. Maybe you'd like to help me, Grover.

I feel like some ice cream, don't you? No? You're sleepy? Good. Go to bed. Be sure and brush your teeth first though. You know how much you hate the dentist, ha, ha.

Sleep well. Good night.

He had a dream about his mother. In it she was lying on the chaise longue in their living room as she did so often. Her yellow hair was spread; she was deeply asleep. Coming from her there was a faint, curious odor, like rubbing alcohol but not like that either. It was very sweet and sharp. It made his eyelids sting. His father stood beside her; he was pleading with her to open her eyes and speak to him.

The windows were open and the dusk was pouring in through them. When it reached his mother she sat up and smiled and then all of this scenery changed.

Beside a lake a garden blew and up some stairs he saw her legs go running. His father cried out and ran after her but the stairs were too quick for him. They moved out into the center of the lake and the water closed over them.

Alone in the dusk-filled chamber he cried out, too, but no one answered. Something squeezed his heart until it panted and he struggled up and awake and wobbled to the window.

Morning's misty hush lay upon the land. The rim of the sun was just sliding into view.

His father had already phoned from Tampa to say that everything was under control there. His dream and yesterday's fear slid away from him.

Ellen Grae came and stayed for breakfast—waffles and cantaloupe. Aunt Marty told him to eat hearty and so he did but just as he was finishing up on his third waffle something funny happened. Suddenly there was this gasp and then this thrusting around his middle and he looked down and lifted the tail of his shirt and saw that his stomach had worked its way out of his clothes.

With her spoon poised above her slice of melon Ellen Grae coldly said, "How disgusting. Put it back or at least cover it up. I'm trying to eat."

He laid his hand on the brown velvet tire. It sighed. He said, "That's funny. It's never done this before. What you reckon's wrong with it?"

"A boy with a fat stomach," said Ellen Grae with an iron look. "If you only knew how awful it looked, fat like that in just one place. The least you could do is exercise and try to spread it around some."

Gently the tire breathed. He covered it with his shirt tail. "It feels heavy. Maybe I've got some kind of disease. Elephantiasis or something like that. There's *some* reason my stomach's pooched out like this all of a sudden. Hey, I wonder if I'm maybe a diabetic and don't know it. That's the way they do, you know. Some of 'em get real skinny and some of 'em get real fat before they find out they're diabetics. Or maybe it's my glands."

Ellen Grae took a dainty bite of her cantaloupe. "I just can't stand fat people. They nauseate me."

"I'm not fat," protested Grover. "Just my stomach is."

"They wheeze."

"I don't wheeze."

"And their flesh is cold."

"My flesh isn't cold."

Ellen Grae fixed a flat, black stare. "And they're sluggish."

"I'm not sluggish. Lookit this. Look at how I can suck this in if I want to. It's got muscle."

Aunt Marty and Uncle Ab both stood up to look. Uncle Ab said, "Yessir, it *has* got muscle. Boy, I wish I could get rid of *my* paunch that easily."

"Yeah," said Grover. "Lookit this. Look how I can get rid of this if I want to. See? It's all gone now. But here it is back again. Now you see it, now you don't. Look, Ellen Grae. Lookit this."

She wouldn't look. "It makes me think of Ramona Gookizen," she said to Aunt Marty. "Ramona's in my grade at school and she isn't modest one bit. When we have physical ed she always changes to her gym clothes in front of me and her stomach looks just like Grover's except hers is white. You know what it reminds me of? A dead fish that's been left in the sun. She wears a corset with her regular clothes. You should see it. It takes me and two other girls fifteen minutes to get her back into it once she takes it off. One day we got her back into it too tight and she fainted and Miss Daniels sent her home with a note to her mother not to let her wear it any more but she still does. Some *men* wear corsets when they get fat, did you know that? Grace told me that so I know it's true. Imagine a man in a corset. It revulses me just to think of it, doesn't it you?"

Aunt Marty said yes, it revulsed her.

After breakfast Grover and Ellen Grae pedaled to town on his bicycle to get Aunt Marty two spools of tan thread and in front of the Western Union office Ellen Grae, who was in charge of the brakes, slammed them on so hard and so suddenly that Grover almost fell off.

Pointing, Ellen Grae said, "Look, Grover. Western Union wants a boy to deliver messages part-time."

"Yeah. Well, I hope they can find one. Come on, the Fair Store's down in the next block. Western Union doesn't sell thread."

Ellen Grae looked at him like he was her husband. "I

don't think it would be hard work. Naturally I'd help you. Come on, let's go see about it."

"See about me being a Western Union boy? You crazy? I don't know anything about being a Western Union boy. Besides I don't want to. Now wait a minute, Ellen Grae!"

"Oh, hush. You can't park out here in the middle of the street. Somebody'll run over you. I'm just . . . Grover, do you mind? I'm trying to park this thing. Honestly. You'd think I was trying to . . . You'll have to get off, Grover. I know it's asking a lot but . . . There, see? Now we're all set."

"Ellen Grae, now I've already told you once I didn't want to . . . Listen, you're not my boss!"

"I know that, Grover. I'm not trying to be. I'm just trying to help you. You're just lucky I didn't take you to a doctor. He'd put you on a diet and *make* you lose all that ugly, unhealthy fat you've taken on. Oh, heck, you should have worn some shoes but maybe Miss Rogers won't look at your feet. Smooth your hair; it's sticking up in the back. And try to look intelligent. Don't suck your cheeks like that; it makes you look like you don't know what you're doing. And hold your stomach in but don't let your pants . . . Oh, there's Miss Rogers. Yoohoo! Miss Rogers!"

Miss Rogers had a faded, crepe-paper mouth and a cloud of fluffy, white hair. Her eyes weren't dry the way some old eyes are. She made Grover think of a bar of Ivory soap. She had a clear, unspotted voice.

She said, "Let's see now. Just which one of you is applying for the job?"

"He is," said Ellen Grae. "His name is Grover Ezell. Tell Miss Rogers your name, Grover."

"My name is Grover Ezell," he said. "But I don't want—"

"Maybe you know his father," cut in Ellen Grae. "He's an electrician for the electric company. And I *know* you know his uncle, Dr. Ezell, Thicket's most beloved veterinarian. If you need any other recommendations I or Mr. and Mrs. McGruder will give them to you. Or Sheriff Fudge. Grover needs the job, Miss Rogers. He'd be a very earnest employee."

With her gold pencil Miss Rogers drew a square box on a blank telegraph pad. Then she put a man inside the box. "Well, I don't know. It would only be in case of emergencies, like this morning. Perhaps you were looking for something a little steadier, Grover?"

"No, ma'am," he answered. "I wasn't looking for anything steadier. To tell you the truth I wasn't looking for anything. I work for my uncle when he needs me and that's the only job I've got time for. I just came downtown today for two spools of thread so's Aunt Marty can let out some of my pants. Miss Rogers, I thank you for your time and all but I—"

"Excuse me," said Miss Rogers, as a machine in the back of the room began to clack, and got up and scurried back to it and when it stopped chattering, lifted her hands like a pianist, placed them on the keys, and hammered out a message of her own.

"That's a teletype machine," informed Ellen Grae. "What are you looking at me like that for? I'm only trying to help you. This job will be good for you, Grover. Riding a bicycle is one of the best exercises there is. In just no time you'll lose your fat stomach and besides we'll get paid for it."

"*We'll* get paid for it!" Grover exclaimed.

"Yes. Don't quibble with her about the price though. Take whatever she offers. You and I can talk about my share later."

"*Your* share!"

"It won't be much. It won't be anything if you don't want it to be. Here she comes. Try to look intelligent now."

He didn't but got hired anyway. It only took about two minutes. He was issued the tools he'd need; one ball-point pen and two pencils and a visored cap with Western Union printed in yellow letters on the front of it. He pointed out his dirty, bare feet but Miss Rogers said that people in Thicket weren't much on protocol and that they wouldn't matter. She asked him if he could start to work right that minute and Ellen Grae said that they could. He phoned Aunt Marty to tell her what had happened, Miss Rogers then showed him how to have customers sign for telegrams and handed him two to be delivered. Then he and Ellen Grae went back out into the street and climbed up on to his bicycle.

"You'll have to drive," he said. "My vision's kind of hampered on account of this cap's too big. Let's see; we've got two places to go. Out to Miss Hasty's and to the Gookizens."

Astride the back end of the bicycle Ellen Grae swung her legs and rolled her eyes. "Grover, we got you this job so *you* could get the exercise. I don't need any. If I do all the pedaling how are you going to lose that stomach fat? Turn your cap around. You heard Miss Rogers say that protocol didn't matter much. She won't care if the Western Union sign is in the back. Let's go."

Sheriff Fudge came out of the barber shop, leaned against the striped pole, and watched them depart.

Along First Street where the trees, goateed with Spanish moss, were sparse, it was searingly hot. Mr. Sangster came out of his green-awninged store and gave them his grocer's smile. The flag atop the post office fluttered limply.

Miss Hasty's place was quite a distance beyond where the paved streets and sidewalks ended. They had to walk through a long stretch of burning sand and then a tangle of blackberry briar to reach their destination but finally they stood before Miss Hasty's door. Grover put his thumb on the bell-button and heard it hollowly ring inside. He had to do it three times before Miss Hasty came. She had a paper bag on her head and smelled like guavas.

At her invitation they stepped inside while she read her telegram which was from G. C., her brother in Baltimore. That it agitated her some she freely admitted. Tucking her lavender mouth she said, "Wouldn't you think a grown man, married and all, would have sense enough to handle his own financial problems?"

"Yes'm," answered Grover. "Looks to me like he would. You want to sign for your telegram, please, Miss Hasty?"

Miss Hasty's hands had sprinkles of brown spots on the backs of them. She fixed him with a sharp, shiny stare. "A man is the most worthless creature alive, Grover, and don't you ever forget it."

She gave Grover and Ellen Grae each a small jar of freshly-made guava jelly to take home.

Trundling back into town they passed Friendship

cemetery and stopped for a little walk through it. Tony, the gravedigger, was there. Grover wasn't watching where he was going and almost fell into the hole Tony was digging.

Despite the gloom of his trade, Tony had a big, cheerful appetite for people and things. To anyone that would listen he was always saying that it was his aim to enjoy everything while he could, even pain and work. He was always saying that he'd seen a lot of people wait for that vague, distant day when they'd have time to be happy and that he'd seen a lot of them get fooled. It wasn't his intention, he said, to join that sorry horde.

He climbed up out of his hole and sat on a mound of freshly disturbed earth and grinned at Ellen Grae and Grover. "Now you take this poor old soul I'm diggin' this hole for," he said. "Eighty-three years old and just never took the time out to enjoy herself. She was always worried about what was gonna happen next week or next year. She worried over the durndest things. One time she hired me to paint her house for her. She said she wanted it a color that'd make her feel good when she looked at it and left it up to me so I had the paint store mix up eight gallons of pretty, bright yellow and two gallons of apple green. Well sir, I got the front all painted nice and fresh and she was happier'n a pig in the sunshine with it but then three of her young 'uns came and each of them had something sour to say about it. So finally, after a lot of fussing and haranguing she had me take all of that nice, pretty paint back to the store and have it made over into the ugliest mud-colored brown you ever saw. She hated that brown color but her kids was satisfied. Poor old soul," he said and jumped back down into his hole and started flinging dirt again.

There were some people in Thicket who didn't like Tony. Ramona Gookizen was one of them.

Ramona was one of those people that Tony talked about. She was always preparing herself for something future. That day it was for a trip to Chicago which she might get to take later on in the summer. From her hairline to her chin she was smeared with a thick, tan paste. She smelled like yeast. Grover asked her what the smell was caused from and she gave him a pale, stiff look and said, "Oh, really, Grover."

Ellen Grae said, "It's yeast. She uses it to draw out the impurities in her skin. She may get to go to Chicago before school starts again and she wants to look nice for it. Give Ramona the telegram, Grover."

Grover handed Ramona the telegram. She opened it, read it, and yawned. "Nothing important," she said. "Are you all thirsty? You look like you are."

Grover and Ellen Grae admitted that they were thirsty and Ramona led them into her kitchen and mixed up some ice and cold tea and grape juice. She wouldn't drink any. She said she didn't like her teeth to turn purple. She said, "No. Fluids make me feel the heat more and I'm already a positive rag. I don't see why Mother and Daddy can't air-condition this house. Just look at all the dust in the air in here. Can you not just imagine what it's doing to our lungs? Having to breathe it all the time? When we lived in Tampa our whole house was air-conditioned. I don't see how people live without it. I just hate Thicket. The people here are so uncouth and there's so much heat and dirt."

Ellen Grae crunched ice, slurped her drink, and gazed at Ramona.

Ramona pulled one of her black, dangling curls around from in back of her ear and rolled it between her fingers. It was straight as a string on the end but she seemed not to notice. "My parents have gone to an auction in St. Petersburg if you can imagine such a thing."

Grover said, "I like auctions. My mother and I went to one once." 1540772

Ramona transferred her gaze from her curl to Grover. "Auctions are cheap and the people who go to them are cheap. Why don't you take that ridiculous cap off, Grover?"

"This cap isn't ridiculous. All Western Union boys wear 'em."

Ramona put the curl back where it had come from and fanned herself with her fingers. "Auctions are cheap and the people that go to them are cheap," she repeated. "I've tried to tell Mother and Daddy that but they won't listen. I suppose they'll come back with some more junk to fill up this dreadful house."

Ellen Grae slid a hunk of ice out of her mouth, salted it, and put it back.

Ramona watched her for a minute then slid her eyes back to Grover. "So your mother took you to an auction once. How quaint."

"Yeah."

"What did you purchase, may I ask?"

"What did we purchase? Well, let me see if I can

remember. Oh, yeah, now I do. We bought a painting by some fella named Van Gogh. You ever heard of him, Ramona?"

The yeast on Ramona's face had dried tight. With a thumb and forefinger she carefully lifted a piece of it away. "Of course. Don't judge everybody by yourself, Grover."

"I'm not. I just wanted to make sure you knew who I was talking about. Van Gogh was the man who invented pork and beans. He just painted in his spare time."

"Grover, I know that. Don't you think I know that? I'm twelve years old and I've seen Van Gogh's pork and beans in grocery stores all my life. But so what? A lot of people invent things. What's so important about pork and beans?"

Grover poked three fingers inside his shirt and gently scratched his stomach. "Nothing, Ramona. Nothing's important about them."

"What are you looking at me like that for? What's so funny?"

"Nothing's funny, Ramona. I'm just . . . I think I've got a toothache. Or maybe a sore tonsil. I sat on some wet ground when we were in the cemetery a few minutes ago and maybe I caught cold in this tonsil. You wouldn't care to have a look at it, would you? And tell me if it's red?"

Ramona made her lip curl. "The cemetery."

"Yeah. Tony was there digging a grave for somebody."

Ramona shuddered, put a hand on her ribs and pressed. "Tony. That dreadful person. Somebody ought to do something about him. He's not decent."

"Tony's not decent? How can you say such a thing, Ramona? Tony's plenty decent."

Anger came into Ramona's haughty face. "He's dreadful. He's not decent. He whistles while he's doing his dreadful work. I've heard him do it and it's not decent. I told my father about hearing him whistle while he digs graves and he agrees with me; it's not decent."

Ramona's opinions, reflected Grover, were tuckering. They'd flat tucker you out if you let them.

His job with Western Union only lasted that one day. When he and Ellen Grae got back to the office about two o'clock Miss Rogers had hired an older, speedier boy to take his place. She gave him a dollar which was more than fair, he thought, for just two telegrams. Ellen Grae refused to take any part of it.

He had forgotten about the thread for his pants and went home without it.

That night he and his Uncle Ab and Aunt Marty drove over to Tampa to see his mother. She had tubes down her nose and throat and was asleep.

His father who was there wouldn't let anyone do anything except stand at the foot of the bed and look.

The room was dim and silent. His father coughed and coughed against his fist and only shook his head in response to whispered questions.

Grover wanted vastly to have his mother open her eyes and look at him but she didn't; she just lay there quietly breathing.

Darkness glittered at the windows. Beyond them, somewhere in the night, a ship's horn blew. A nurse rustled in, looked at his mother, touched her hair, and rustled out again. Aunt Marty and Uncle Ab went with her.

His father turned to him and in a hushed, unnatural voice said, "You go, too, Grover. No sense in your hanging around here. It'll be hours before she wakes up."

Not even one touch was allowed. The hand on his shoulder was firm as they moved toward the door. He heard the ship's horn again and then Aunt Marty had him by the arm and they were walking toward the elevator.

In the car, headed back toward Thicket, he had things explained to him: His mother had had a little cyst removed.

"Removed from where?" he asked.

"Oh, ah, her liver," they answered.

Their voices were soft and breathless. "We didn't tell you before," they said, "because we didn't want you to worry. Wasn't that nice of us? To do your worrying for you?"

"Yes," he said. "That was very nice of you. When is my mother coming home?"

"Oh, in a few days," they answered.

One of them leaned to switch on the radio. The car filled with music. With both hands Aunt Marty lifted her hair from the back of her neck and said how hot it was, said that surely to goodness it would rain soon. Uncle Ab said he thought it would.

He couldn't see their faces because he was in the back seat and there was only the light from the dashboard but he felt . . . something. They were too cheerful, too smooth. And yet not cheerful and smooth at all. Underneath they were solemn and tense.

"What caused the cyst?" he asked after a while.

Uncle Ab's answer came back very fast. "Oh, now Grover, you know what causes cysts. You've seen them in animals. Why harp on something that's over and done? Think about something constructive, why don't you?"

Aunt Marty half turned in her seat, so that he had a dim image of one side of her face, and said, "Oh, before I forget, Grover. I *do* want to get my hydrangeas moved tomorrow. You *will* help me, won't you?"

"Yes'm," he answered. "I'll help you."

Chapter Three

A worry came to Grover and fastened itself on the back of his mind and clung there in a blurred, inky shape. He could name it to himself; sometimes at night when it pressed close, he did. He whispered it to the darkness: "Something is wrong with my mother that they aren't telling me. Maybe she's going to die."

But he couldn't say this to anyone else. He was too afraid of what they would say afterward. So the questions in his mind just hung there like small ghosts. There was his pride. Pride can be stronger than fear; fear can be managed with pride.

Aunt Marty said that in all her born days she had never seen anybody eat with the gusto he did: two helpings of everything washed down with great quantities of milk, iced tea, and water. She said she had never seen anybody sleep so painlessly, that his bed hardly needed making in the morning. She said she had never seen anybody work so tirelessly. In one day he dug six new holes for the hydrangea bushes and helped reset them, washed Aunt Marty's car and Uncle Ab's pickup truck, swept out the garage, and then went with Uncle Ab to treat a sick dog.

The dog, which was a six-year-old male boxer, belonged to Reverend Vance, the Methodist minister. When they got there he was staggering around his doghouse crying with pain. Two neighbors, both of them men, were hanging over the board fence watching. One of them had a shotgun.

Positioned in the screened-in safety of his back porch, Reverend Vance was pretty excited. He said, "Abner, I don't know as I'd go out there if I were you. I'm almost sorry I called you. Obviously the dog is very sick. He might be dangerous."

Uncle Ab shifted his bag from one hand to the other and glanced toward the fence.

The man holding the gun raised it and aimed it at the boxer. "Doc," he hollered. "I think the best thing to do is shoot the dog! He's rabid sure as I'm standing here! They ain't no sense in taking any chances! You and your boy and the Reverend Vance stay right where you are and I'll take care of this!"

Uncle Ab shifted his bag again and looked out across the yard at the boxer. His big, square head was shaking; saliva dripped from his mouth. He appeared to be blind.

Half to himself, Uncle Ab said, "That's not rabies," and pushed the screen door open and started down the steps.

The man with the gun made a menacing motion. "Doc," he hollered. "Better not go near him! He's rabid! Jest you and the boy stand back now! I'll put him out of his misery with just one shot!"

With more authority than Grover had ever seen him

display, Uncle Ab left the steps and went striding out
across the lawn toward the stricken dog. He didn't look
at the man with the gun but he spoke to him in a terrible voice. "Put that gun down, you idiot! This dog's not
rabid. If you want to get over here and help me with
him get over here and do it. If you don't, shut your
mouth and get away from that fence."

Grover was right behind Uncle Ab. They reached the
boxer and the dog swung his head around, trying to
focus his eyes on them but couldn't. Panting and sweat-
ing, he took a couple of steps toward them, stopped,
pawed the air, collapsed, and went into a jerking, twist-
ing convulsion.

Uncle Ab dropped his bag to the ground and knelt
beside it. With one eye on the flailing dog he opened
his bag and stuck his hand inside. It came back out
holding a syringe and two bottles of medicine. "Toad
poisoning," he said. "This is the second case today. You
think you can help me hold him, Grover, and let me get
some of this into him?"

Grover couldn't have held the dog by himself; the
boxer was too big and heavy and his convulsions were
jerking him around quite a bit, but Reverend Vance
came running to help and with not so much trouble
they got twenty milligrams of prednisone and twenty-
five milligrams of propiopromazine hydrochloride into
him. He quieted in just a few minutes; was fully recov-
ered within an hour. Reverend Vance brought an old,
clean blanket and spread it in the doghouse and the
boxer crawled inside and went to sleep.

The men at the fence had disappeared. Uncle Ab
said he hoped the one with the gun would himself bite
a toad one day and get poisoned from it.

They drove home through the murky night and his father was there, nervously waiting for him. He had Grover gather up all his stuff and they went back to their own house to prepare, said Grover's father, for his mother's homecoming.

"Is she all well now?" he asked.

His father coughed against his fist. "Grover, why is it you have to have everything explained to you three or four times? Try washing your ears out once in a while. Maybe you'll be able to hear better."

"My ears are washed out. I wash them out every day. What're you moving the piano for? You're making marks on the floor. Mother won't like it."

His father pushed the piano to the wall, took a tape measure from his pocket and got down on his hands and knees.

"Now what are you doing? What're you measuring the floor for?"

"I'm going to have wall-to-wall carpeting laid in here."

"What for?"

"For your mother. She's always wanted it and now I'm going to get it for her."

"What color?"

"Grover, I don't know what color. Blue, I suppose. That's your mother's favorite."

"It's not mine. Too many things are blue. Everywhere you look something's blue. The sky. Water. People's eyes. You can't look anywhere without seeing something blue. I get tired of it. Black's my favorite color. When something's black you can't tell when it's dirty. Now what are you doing? You going to have wall-to-wall carpeting laid here in the kitchen, too?"

His father showed him tattered patience. "No, Grover, I am not going to have wall-to-wall carpeting laid here in the kitchen. I am measuring to see if a dishwasher will fit in here."

"What dishwasher?"

"The dishwasher I'm going to buy. Why don't you go to bed?"

"It's too early. When are you going to do all this?"

"I'm going to start tomorrow. Where's the key to this china cabinet? Do you know?"

"Yes, sir. It was right here on . . . yeah, here it is."

His father took the key from him and walked to the china cabinet but didn't open it. He laid his hand on its rich, patina front and looked hard through the little glass doors at the assortment inside; the cut glass bowls, the sterling silver coffee service, the platinum-rimmed plates and saucers and cups, all so carefully arranged.

"She likes all that stuff in there," Grover said. "It's about time for it to get washed and polished again. She always does it just before her birthday."

His father made no answer to this. He turned away from the cabinet and went out on the back porch and started rummaging around out there.

It still wasn't Grover's bedtime but he went anyway. Trying to talk to someone who doesn't want to talk to you isn't very comfortable.

There was this time of frantic activity and change— two days of it. A panel truck came and three men in white overalls jumped out of it, rushed into the house, set up ladders, climbed up on them, and started to paint. They said for Grover to stay out of their way, that they were in a hurry. One of them dipped snuff and had to get down every few minutes to go outside and spit.

His father told him to clean up his room and he did but it didn't satisfy him. The second time his father went with him and they threw out two boxes of things it had taken him years to collect. His father said the stuffed owl disgusted him.

Another truck brought a dishwasher and an air-conditioner. His father ordered him not to get in the way of the men who installed them. The air-conditioner went into his mother's bedroom.

"When is she coming home?" Grover asked.

His father turned an exhausted look on him. "Probably day after tomorrow. Haven't you got anything to do besides stand around and bother people?"

Both of his bicycle tires were flat. He had to walk to the McGruders.

Farrell, who was a Pennsylvania Yankee, was crazy about boiled peanuts. The first thing he headed for, each time he came to Thicket was the peanut pot; it didn't matter whose. He'd squat down beside it like a bear feeding on berries, shoveling the nuts into one side of his mouth and getting rid of the shells with the other. He did this until he was glassy-eyed. He'd answer yes or no while he was eating but if more than this was wanted it was best to wait until he was through because anything lengthier just came out garbled.

Grover went up the McGruders' steps and squatted beside Farrell's pile of wet, sucked shells and said, "Hey, Farrell. No, don't try to talk to me now. I can see you're busy. I got lots of time today. I'll just sit here and wait until you're through doing what you're doing."

Farrell blinked his rain-colored eyes and grunted. He said, "Oh. Itchu."

"Yeah," Grover said. "It's me."

Sprawled in the swing with a bowl of peanuts on her stomach and her nose stuck in a book Ellen Grae said, "This is certainly a prolix book. I've been trying to find out for two hours what it's about and haven't yet. I don't know why writers have to hide what stories are about with a lot of other stuff. I'm going to write one someday and I'm going to come right out on the first page and say what it's about. If you want some peanuts, Grover, you'd better hurry."

Grover said he didn't want any peanuts and took a seat on the porch railing.

Farrell moved around to the other side of the peanut pot where the pickings were better. Sunlight filtering through a thick, green panel of vine at his back turned the color of his clipped scalp a gleaming white.

Ellen Grae lowered one of her legs to the floor and gave the swing a push with her bare foot. "The heroine's name in this book is Evangeline. Evangeline. If that doesn't make me sick to my stomach. I don't know why parents give their children such slushy names. You know what it makes me think of? Anemia. It makes me think of a girl in a wheelchair who's anemic. She's in the Belgian Congo helping her father. He's a missionary."

Grover said, "Is that what that book's about, Ellen Grae?"

"No. I'm just making this up. I'm going to write it when I have time and send it away to a magazine and get paid for it. Where was I?"

"Let me see," said Grover. "Evangeline was sitting in

her wheelchair in the Belgian Congo. It was getting dark and she was getting scared 'cause she was all by herself. Everybody else had gone way up into the hills early that morning to talk to the people about their sinful ways. Evangeline was used to the jungle, having been raised in it by her father after an ape twisted her mother's head off two days after she was born, but that night, for some reason, she was queasy. The volcanoes were erupting, that was the reason. Sparks and fire were shooting out of their craters like rockets and hot lava was gushing down, and on the rim of the fiery crater Evangeline thought she could make out the outline of a woman with a baby strapped to her back. Suddenly the woman ran forward and jumped. She screamed when she did it and Evangeline, shaking and quaking in her wheelchair, screamed too for coming toward her out of the black jungle there was this big gorilla. He had a hellish face and was making the most gosh-awful sounds Evangeline had ever heard. She felt all of her blood coagulate. It froze right in her veins."

"She didn't have much of it," reminded Ellen Grae. "She was anemic, don't forget."

"Oh, yeah, that's right. Well, what little bit she did have froze in her veins. The pathologist who performed the autopsy on her said he'd never seen anything like it. The blood in the aorta was as solid as a rock. He had to slice—"

"The blood in what, Grover?" asked Ellen Grae.

"In the aorta. That's the big blood vessel in your heart. It starts at the left ventricle and puts blood to every part of your body through branches."

"Grover, I know about the aorta. You've explained it to me many times. I'm just trying to find out . . . are we

still talking about Evangeline? Was it her aorta that
was frozen solid as a rock?"

"Sure. That's who we're talking about, isn't it?
Evangeline?"

Ellen Grae laid her book aside and sat up. "Dying,"
she sighed. "All you talk about lately is somebody
dying. Do you realize that, Grover? What's the matter
with you?"

"Nothing."

"You sure?"

"Yeah."

"You don't look like you're sure. Are you worried
about something?"

"I might be but it isn't anything you can help me
with. I don't want to talk about it," answered Grover.

A butterfly with brilliant orange dots on its body fluttered out from the vine beyond Farrell's head, winged
to a bush beside the steps, settled on a white, deep-
throated blossom, stuck its head inside and sucked at
the nectar there.

Farrell had finished with the peanuts. With a regret-
ful look he piled all of the empty shells on a square of
newspaper, grunted to his feet, hugged himself, looked
at Grover and said, "There. Now I'm ready."

There was no sense in trying to convince Farrell that
not everybody pined for his company. He knew better.
He always said, "Oh, now, lambie, you know you like
me. Come on, let's go."

Farrell was canny but he hid being that way. That
day when Grover and Ellen Grae took him down to the
river and steered him away from the spot where
Grover's boat was tied he got very excited. He said that
anybody who would steal the only thing three little

kids had to have summer fun with was nothing but a big blob of scum, lower than a viper's belly. A vulture, a fiend, an ugly old ghoul. "Curses on him!" he cried. "I'd run him through if he was here! I'd cut out his old gizzard and make him eat it! I'd set his old bare rump on an anthill! Oh, I'd fix him, I would!"

Grover said, "Yeah. Well, there's no sense in getting all excited about it now, Farrell. The boat's been gone three or four days now and Ellen Grae and I are about worn out worrying over it. It's gone. Just plain gone. Where you going? Home?"

Hugging himself, Farrell skipped around in a wide circle, brandishing his make-believe sword. "Avast there, matey! Knuckle your forelock when addressing me, sir, else I clap you in irons! You low-down skunk! I'll teach you to thieve! Take that! And that!"

Ellen Grae and Grover sat down on a fallen log and tried not to look at Farrell. Grover said, "Don't watch him, Ellen Grae. He'll get tired in a minute and go home."

Ellen Grae propped her legs, sighed, and opened her book which she'd brought along. "Chapter two. Evangeline had better do something pretty quick or I'm going to ditch her. Here she is bawling again. I thought I got through with all her misery in the first chapter but no, she's still at it."

Grover watched Farrell's robust legs carry him out of their clearing. Darting from tree to tree he disappeared altogether in a moment.

"He's gone," said Ellen Grae without looking up.

"Yeah."

"Do you think we fooled him about the boat?"

"Sure. He believed us. Yankees aren't very smart.

They'll believe anything. That's why they're always in such a rush. You ever noticed the way Yankees walk, Ellen Grae?"

"No. That's one thing that's never interested me. Please stop scratching yourself, Grover. You're making me nervous. I'm trying to finish this chapter."

"What's Evangeline doing now? Not that I want to know."

"She's pouring tea for her father. He's trying to ignore her grief."

"What's she grieving about?"

"I don't know. She wants to marry a commoner and he doesn't want her to."

"What's a commoner?"

With a contained look Ellen Grae closed the book. "Grover, what a commoner is has got nothing to do with us. I'll explain it to you some other time. What are we going to do? Just sit here all day with our minds blank?"

"My mind isn't blank. Yours might be but mine isn't. I was thinking about doing some fishing now that we got rid of Farrell."

Ellen Grae stood up and gave a hitch to her pants. "Okay, let's go."

All around them, the drowsing swamp buzzed and hummed in the heat of midmorning. The river was a streamer of brown glass. In its wetness a cluster of water hyacinths stirred, dipping their pale heads.

"They don't do that by themselves," said Ellen Grae. "Something's underneath making them move. What are we stopping here for? The boat's on down a ways."

Grover said, "No, it isn't. If you'd care to have a look

you'll see it coming around the bend. Farrell's in it. Look."

Ellen Grae looked and said, "Well, I'll be dipped. I sure will be dipped."

Farrell had caught them in their lie but he didn't say a word about it. Seated in the center of the boat with the sun full on him he came cracking around the bend with such speed and energy that even Ellen Grae was moved to admiration. "Look at him!" she exclaimed. "I didn't know he was that strong!"

Farrell was enjoying himself. Out of a piece of old newspaper he had made himself a tricornered hat and out of a length of Spanish moss he had made himself a sash which was knotted around his waist. He had made a jaunty ascot and a set of elbow-length cuffs out of more moss. He wore a monocle cut from a piece of bark.

Pluming a lane of foaming wake he plowed up to where he was abreast of Ellen Grae and Grover, laid down his oar, stood up, adjusted his monocle, addressed his crew. "Steady as she goes there, matey! Belay the belay! Luff those lines there, me good ruddies! Run up the colors! Man the shrouds! Sound general quarters!"

Staring at him Ellen Grae said, "I'll be dipped. Outsmarted by a Yankee."

Pretending not to notice them, Farrell climbed up on the boat's center board, smote his forehead, waved his arms, and screamed directions. "Avast there, matey! Up the ladder! Up the ladder, man, and be quick about it! What's that? A European man-of-war you say? How big? Matey, it don't matter at a time like this how many guns she's got! One's enough! Abandon ship! Abandon ship! Abandon ship!"

Together Matey and Farrell abandoned ship. Matey drowned but Farrell made it to shore. In their clothes Ellen Grae and Grover had to swim out and get the boat. Farrell said he was too winded to help. He arranged himself on a mound of green moss and languidly watched.

Altogether this day was not one which rightfully could be called a success. On the way home Grover stepped on a board with a rusty nail in it and when his father saw the wound he turned red angry. He demanded to know if Grover ever watched where he was going and wanted to know what was wrong with wearing shoes once in a while and sent him off to the doctor to get a tetanus shot. In the doctor's office he had to wait two hours for his turn to come. The man sitting on the settee beside him had blackened teeth and smelled of old sweat. He made Grover's head ache.

And then when he got home he found his father standing in the middle of his mother's room. He had his hands in his face and was crying. At some sound Grover made he turned and his bruised eyes rested but he was unable to speak.

My father, Grover thought and the whole of their relationship—being related but never friends—fell on him. He wanted to speak to his father, to say something that would benefit them both but there was silence between them and in the end all they spoke about was the tetanus shot—how much it had hurt and how long he had had to wait to get it. They didn't speak of the other—the reason for the tears.

But he knew. He knew then that there was much more to it than just a cyst which had been removed.

And that night, lying in the bland darkness he said it aloud for the first time: "She's going to die. My mother is going to die." Testing the words for the truth that was in them and hearing it there.

Chapter Four

His mother came home and in the first days of the three of them being together again there was a climate of relief and nothing more.

She said she didn't hurt anywhere and she didn't act like she did. She took off her shoes and in her bare feet walked around on the new carpet, showing her pleasure. She said how wonderful the controlled coolness of her bedroom was and that she'd rather have the dishwasher than a diamond tiara.

His father hired a woman to come in twice a week to do the heavy cleaning and his mother wryly allowed this but she would not allow his father to make trips home from his job just to check on how things were at home. She said, "No, we each have a job. Let's do them."

She was thin but not gaunt and now when Grover looked at her, watched her small, sprightly occupations, he said to himself, "It isn't so. It was all in my imagination. They were telling me the truth; it *was* only a cyst. Now it's gone and she's well."

And so the fear melted and temporarily slipped away.

At night and on Sundays his father pampered her and with this new, odd smile she had she accepted his attentions, let him bring her glasses of water, the newspaper, a footstool. But all she wanted from Grover was his company:

"Where are you going, Grover?"

"Fishing. You seen my tackle box?"

"It's in the closet on the back porch. How about some breakfast before you go sailing off?"

"I ate with Dad. You see this bug? I made it. You see the way I've got the feathers on it tied? They'll splay in the water. This here bug is going to make a lot of bass mad. Maybe I'll try to patent it but first I got to try it out to make sure it works the way I think it's going to. What's the matter? What're you looking at me like that for?"

She put her hands in the pockets of her short, white dress. "No reason. I just thought you'd like to stay here with me today."

A hundred times she asked him to do that—to stay and sit with her in the warm, yellow kitchen. They'd drink iced tea and she'd talk to him about the places she'd lived, his grandparents Ezell (both dead), his grandparents Cornett (also both dead), a great-aunt named Jenny (alive in Council Bluffs, Iowa), a man she'd been in love with before she married his father.

As she talked she polished things. "Someday you'll be in love, Grover. Have you ever thought about that?"

"Naaaaaah. Not me. You're never gonna catch *me* in that agony. I'm going to be a bachelor. Is that the pickle dish that cost twenty-five dollars?"

"Yes, it is. Isn't it lovely?"

"It's okay. Why didn't you marry that other man? The one before my father?"

"Oh, there were several reasons. Our religions were different for one thing."

"What other reason? What else was wrong with him?"

His mother dipped a corner of her rag into a jar of silver cream and ran it around the base of the pickle dish. "Grover, his religion wasn't a fault. No religion with anyone is."

"Okay, okay, I know that. I should. You've told me a thousand times. But what else was wrong with him?"

Beneath her fingers the pickle dish had taken on a rich, satiny sheen. She lifted it to the light, examining it for streaks. "He didn't have any humor in him," she said. "Not one speck. I couldn't possibly have married him. A sense of humor is one of the most important things in the whole world, Grover."

"Yes'm."

Strangely tender, her smile drifted toward him. "You don't know what I'm talking about, do you? But that's all right. Someday you will. There isn't any better defense against life than a sense of humor. You just remember that I said that."

He said, "Yes'm, I will." But the promise was vague. It wasn't important.

There was sun at the windows and beyond them a swirl of color and smell and sound, a sweep of scarlet wings in the cajeput trees along the back fence, the sweet, heady scent of Cape jasmine, a soft swoosh of wind.

Finished with the pickle dish his mother turned her attention to a tray of small spoons.

He said, "If you had married that other man probably I would have been like him but maybe not. I'm not like Dad."

Her pale fingers lifted one of the spoons. "No, you're not. You're a Cornett more than you are an Ezell. We knew you were going to be the day you were born."

"How'd you know it?"

The bowl of the spoon disappeared into the blackened cloth. "Because you didn't howl. You never howled about anything. You just laid in your crib and waited to be changed or fed or picked up. We thought it was the funniest thing. We thought you might be sick and lugged you around from doctor to doctor trying to find out but of course we never did because there wasn't a thing wrong with you. You were just born more Cornett than Ezell, that was all."

"Cornetts don't howl about things, huh?"

Cleaned of its tarnish the spoon came out of the cloth, was laid beside the pickle dish.

Her chin above the starched whiteness of her collar was strong. She said, "That's right; we don't howl about things. There's really no sense in howling, you know. It doesn't do a bit of good. And on top of that it takes a lot of energy. A lot of it. And people don't sympathize. Sometimes they care but this can only help you up to a certain point. Then you've got to go it alone. Depend on your own gumption and common sense."

He said, "Yes'm."

"Grover," his mother said and her voice was cobbled, like footsteps on uneven stones. "Grover, I want to tell you something about your father."

"Ma'am?"

"Your father," she said and now her voice was even. She took up another of the spoons, dipped her rag in the silver cream and polished. "I want to tell you something about him I'm sure you don't know. Are you listening?"

"Yes'm, I'm listening."

"I don't want you to laugh. You won't, will you?"

"No, I won't laugh."

Her eyes were very clear and very brilliant. With the back of her hand she pushed at her hair. Through the thin stuff of her sleeve the flesh of her upper arm looked clean and firm. She said, "Your father is such a fine man, Grover. You believe that, don't you?"

"Yes."

"He's very strong. He's equal. That's what I'm trying to say."

"Equal?"

"To any situation. He's equal to any situation, that's what I mean to say."

This conversation didn't seem to him to be connected with anything. He wondered why they were having it.

Some faint color had come into her cheeks and suddenly her eyes were shy. "In a minute," she said, "I'm going to let you go. I know you're not enjoying this."

He lied. He said, "Yes, I am. I don't mind it a bit. I wasn't gonna do anything this morning except try out my new bug. It can wait. I don't even know if it'll work or not. Want me to fix us some more tea? This is kind of watery."

She glanced at him and then quickly looked away. "No, I don't want any more tea. I just want to . . . well, while we're sitting here like this just talking I just thought I might try to make you understand some things about your father you may not know. And may not ever discover by yourself."

He didn't know that it was a serious moment, one that he would remember. He only felt its unimportance. To hasten its life he said, "I understand what you mean. You don't have to tell me. My father is a fine man. He's equal to any situation."

"Yes," said his mother and after that let him go.

He took his new bug down to the river and sure enough it performed just as he had pictured in his mind it would. It casted accurately. After a little practice it did everything he had hoped it would. With its hackle feathers wiggling it shimmied and popped and skittered, raising the ire of one crafty old bugger to such a pitch that he almost forgot himself and climbed up into the boat with Grover.

He remembered this day for two reasons. Because of his bug and its success and because of the conversation with his mother.

These things and others like them took place in the good days when life was enjoyable and endeared and respected.

But then there came the bad ones.

The three of them went to a beach one weekend because she said she wanted the salt air and water. They would flow into her bones, she said, and increase her strength.

They stayed in a cabana named Contentment. Its roof was made out of artificial palm fronds. At its back there was a long stretch of private, white sand. In the early mornings this was cool and moist. They walked along its shore and gathered shells and fed the gulls and he and his father swam in the blue-green surf but his mother only waded in the shallows. Just the gentle push of the water tired her and made her knees ache, she said. She apologized for this.

They went to an open-air restaurant one night and sat at a round table beneath a kapok tree and ate hot, buttered lobster and cold, boiled shrimp. It was good but in the middle of it they had to leave.

It was just a little nausea, she said, with her eyes suddenly gone sick and her hands pressed. It would go away. She would just go out to the car and lie down for a minute. No need for all of their suppers to be ruined.

Grover watched her wobble to the door. His father had his billfold out and was gesturing to the waiter. They went back to the cabana and his mother went to bed though it was way too early for that.

They went home the next day and his mother walked around touching things and said, "Ah, this is the best place of all." And Uncle Ab and Aunt Marty came with an iced watermelon and they took it out into the back and ate it.

On top things were as they had always been. His father went to work in the mornings and came home from it in the afternoon. He yelled at Grover about things: his unfulfilled promise to rid the lawn of sandspurs, his filthy body, his addiction to fishing. He was used to it; it didn't bother him. It bothered him when his father *didn't* yell. When he just sat with his newspaper folded to the same page and stared at it for thirty minutes, not reading a word of it. Or left his bed in the middle of the night and walked around outside just in his slippers and pajamas.

Silent as a burglar there came this feeling that they were waiting for something.

People came and brought things. They stayed longer, especially if it was in the afternoon and the women, making coffee in the kitchen, whispered together as they set out cups and sliced cake.

The housekeeping woman now came four times a week instead of two and sometimes stayed to cook supper and clean up afterward. She scowled when Grover told her nobody would eat her corned-beef hash if she put milk in it. She said, "Huh. That's all *you* know. Which you think they'd like better with it? Biscuits or cornbread?"

"Cornbread. You see this watch?"

"Yu, yu."

"It's fifty years old. My uncle gave it to me."

"Yu?"

"I didn't ask him for it. He just did. What you reckon made him?"

"Maybe he figures you should learn how to tell time."

"Haw. I knew how to tell time when I was four years old. Where do you live?"

"In a house."

"Where in a house?"

"Lutie Lane."

"Where the garbage dump is?"

"Yu."

"Why do you say yu instead of yes?"

"I don' know. Maybe because I used to work for
some German people. That's what they said. Yu. Yu."

"You live in your house by yourself?"

"Yu, yu."

He watched her measure baking powder into a mix-
ing bowl. Her empty mouth counted: One, two, three,
four.

The watch in his hand ticked off the seconds. Made
in Switzerland, its case was solid gold. A gentleman, his
grandfather Ezell had worn it tucked into the little
waist pocket of his vest for almost fifty years. Its chain
looked like solid gold, too. This was a superior watch, a
piece that any boy should be proud to own.

The woman who shared the still, steamy warmth of
the scrubbed kitchen with him had a closed face. The
eyes in it didn't say anything. Among the cornbread
ingredients, her hands were slow. She measured and
counted everything. One-eighth teaspoon of salt, one
teaspoon of sugar, three tablespoons of melted butter.
"Egg," she said to herself and shuffled to the refrigerator to get it.

He said, "My name's Grover."

She shuffled back to the table. "Yu, yu."

"What's yours?"

"Rose."

"Rose what?"

"Jus' Rose."

"It's a pretty name."

Rose grunted. "Milk," she said, and shuffled back to
the refrigerator.

He said, "Rose is one of the prettiest names there is.
I like people named after flowers: Rose, Daisy, Violet.
If I ever get to be a father I'm going to name all my

children after flowers. The girls, I mean. I forgot Columbine. That's the name of a Western flower. Of course it isn't as pretty as Rose but it's different."

The milk was on the lowest shelf. Rose had to lean over to get it.

He said, "My mother likes cornbread. Probably she'll like your hash, too. We'll probably eat it all."

"Probably," muttered Rose and shuffled back with the carton of milk.

The watch in his palm was smooth and cool. "My mother likes you. So does my father. So do I."

"That's good. I like to have people like me."

He made his voice loose and easy so she wouldn't know how important the question was he had come to ask. "What's wrong with my mother, Rose?"

"What you mean?"

"I mean why does she stay in bed so much? I thought maybe you could tell me."

"Well, I can't," said Rose, measuring milk. "She had an operation. That's all I know."

"Did *you* ever have an operation?"

"Yu."

"What for?"

"Gall bladder."

"How long did *you* have to stay in bed?"

"Long time."

"How long?"

"I don't know. I forgot. But long time."

They ate the hash. It wasn't so bad. Rose was smugly pleased.

Grover's mother was a little wounded bird. She seemed so helpless but sometimes when she thought nobody was watching her she'd lift her chin and make her shoulders square and all the softness would leave her. She'd look strong.

She liked him to look at things with her. She said, "Come look at the wind, Grover."

"What wind?"

"There in the clouds. Ah, I love it. It's eternal and alive. Think of what the world would be like without the wind."

"It's just air moving around."

"Yes," she agreed with odd disappointment. "Yes, that's true." She turned from the doorway and came back to her couch. "I'm tired," she sighed and settled herself on the white pillows and went to sleep.

Rose came in and covered her feet with a light, clean blanket. They looked chilly.

Later on, remembering Rose doing that for his mother, made him ache; made him say to himself: Oh, I wish I had thought to do that for her. I wish that I had. And to show her my watch and agree with her about the wind.

Because the next day she was dead.

He was down on the river with Ellen Grae and Farrell when it happened.

They said she killed herself with a gun. They wouldn't let him look at her room or even go down the hallway past it to his own.

His father was someone he had never seen before. He shouted at Aunt Marty and called Uncle Ab and the doctor terrible names and slammed out of the house and ran around in senseless circles in the yard until Uncle Ab went out and slapped him and forced him to stop.

Aunt Marty and the doctor stood in the living room and talked in low tones.

Rose took him into the kitchen with her and bent and put her rough cheek against his. "Poor little shaver," she crooned. "Poor little shaver."

Her breath smelled like sauerkraut.

✳ Chapter Five

There was a funeral.

The deep, rich organ music drowned them in a river of sorrow and was hideous. The fragrance from the banks of flowers, extravagantly red and yellow and pink, was suffocating. A blanket of red roses with a cross of white gardenias in its center covered the closed casket.

Knotted uncomfortably in their hard pews the people softly breathed and sighed. A woman in a hat shaped like a warrior's helmet stared at him. Her eyes were like dark jelly.

At the lectern Reverend Vance read from Psalms with pure, heavy grace. The words flowed from his mouth as if they were molded.

In this time each of them, he and his father, were alone. His father did not look at him or touch him. His father did not cry or cough or make any sound. He was like stone.

Uncle Ab and Aunt Marty and Rose were there. Rose's brown silk dress had a shower of colored beads on its front. Her slip showed. Uncle Ab and Aunt Marty sat with their hands in their laps and looked straight ahead.

After the passages from Psalms a lady with a clear, stylish voice stood in her pew and read a poem about sunsets and evening stars. Then the minister said a prayer and then everybody filed out of the church and got in their cars and drove to the cemetery.

In an eerie lavender haze the people gathered around the gravesite. Grover glanced at his father and saw the bleached face, saw it stiffen when the little company started to sing "Nearer My God to Thee."

Still covered with its flower blanket the casket was lowered into the earth. Reverend Vance prayed. Grover's father took a step backward, and shook off an outstretched hand.

He saw Rose covertly trying to fix her slip. Her canvas shoes weren't good enough for her dress. One of them had a vertical slit over the second toe. Her feet hurt her, he thought. That's why she didn't wear better ones.

It was over. Reverend Vance wanted to go home with them but Grover's father said, "No, no. Not now. I don't want that now."

Looking appeased and solemn the funeral director and his helpers drove away in their black car.

Uncle Ab and Aunt Marty drove them home. When they got there they started to get out of the car and come in but his father said, "Oh, let us alone for a while. Just let us alone." And pushed Grover out ahead of him and with an iron expression strode around the lawn turning on the sprinklers. The last one drenched him and he came into the house and wiped the water

from his face and hair but didn't change his shirt or coat. He said, "Are you hungry, Grover?"

"No, sir."

His father sat in his chair and held his hands the way a woman does when she's in pain. "Well, there's just the two of us now."

"Yes, sir."

"It'll take a while to get used to it. It isn't going to be easy."

"No, sir."

His father put his hands on his knees and then moved them to the arms of his chair. A tight, economical look lay across the surface of his eyes but in back of it something wavered. "Rose . . . I spoke with Rose. She'll come every day now. Not today though. I didn't want her here today."

Grover looked at the dove-gray wall beyond his father's head. Somebody had left a smudged thumbprint. Their hands weren't clean, he thought. He said, "Rose is nice. I like her. I asked her what her last name was but she wouldn't tell me. She said it was just Rose. Do you know what her last name is?"

His father wrapped his right fist in his left one. The control in his eyes gave way. "Her last name? My aching back, what difference does it make? At a time like this what earthly difference does it make?"

"It doesn't make any difference, Dad. I just wondered."

The dark eyes were turned on him and the discipline began falling away in pieces. All of him took part in this; his eyebrows, his mouth, his face and neck muscles, his breath. The tears came pouring out of his eyes and he didn't wipe them away. He put his head back and his chest rose and fell. "Grover, it was an accident. She knew she was sick but . . . it was an accident. Don't let anyone ever tell you that it was anything else. You hear me?"

"Yes, sir."

Under the smooth, fine whiteness of his shirt his father's ribs heaved and within the brown casing of his throat there took place a terrible struggle. "Ahhhhhhh," he said, pushing the words out. "Ahhhhhhh. This isn't justice. There isn't any justice. It isn't fair. Can you say that this is fair? Ahhhhhhh. Ahhhhhhh."

It's some kind of a test, Grover thought. He wants me to say that it isn't fair and that part's all right but it wasn't an accident. She was sick, awful sick. And she didn't want . . . No, I don't know what she didn't want. I'm just guessing. But it wasn't an accident. She did it. But I can't say that to him. It would make him mad. He wants me to say that I know it was an accident. He wants me to think that she climbed up and got the gun from that storage place on the back porch and carried it to her room just to look at it and it went off accidentally, but that isn't so.

Lost in his pain and loneliness his father had turned sideways in his chair. He had his hands crossed on his chest and was fiercely hugging himself. "Ahhhhhhh," he said. "Ahhhhhhh."

Grover didn't know what to say to his father. They weren't together. It was just being there in the same room at the same time that made it seem like they were.

He deserted the house by the side door and walked around and sat on the white stone bench beneath the persimmon tree. The lawn sucked thirstily at the water from the sprinklers. He thought about death. What it was. God, maybe. Or Time. The Time to cast away time like in Ecclesiastes. Or maybe it was space.

My father shouldn't cry that way in front of me, he thought. He shouldn't. I don't cry in front of him.

And then he thought, it wasn't an accident. It was her trouble and that was her way to get out of it.

Chapter Six

Rose couldn't read. Grover asked her where she was originally from and she said, "Jacksonville?" As if she wasn't certain.

So he said, "Show me on the map."

And with a look of mirth and secrecy she walked her fingers around the map, selected first Boston, then Houston.

He said, "That's not Jacksonville. That's Houston."

"Is it? Well, maybe I made a mistake. Maybe Houston's where I'm from."

"You can't read, can you?"

"Not exactly."

"That's funny."

"You think so? You'd change your mind if you couldn't."

"I meant peculiar. Can you write?"

Rose had taken to wearing hibiscus blossoms in her grizzled hair. Dusted thick inside with pollen, the bright, fluted bells didn't last long but Rose seemed not to mind when they collapsed. She patted them when she didn't have anything else to do with her hands, which wasn't often. That morning they were pink. And fresh because it was early. She patted them and to answer his question asked one of her own. "Now how can I write if I don't know how to read?"

"I don't know. I just thought . . . hey, I just had an idea. I could teach you how to read. It'd be easy."

Rose patted the hibiscus blossoms again. A little puff of pollen drifted out of one of them and settled on her eyebrows. She said, "You think so? How would you do that?"

"Well, I'd start by teaching you the alphabet. Unless you already know it. Do you?"

"Do I what?"

"Know the alphabet."

"What's alphabet?"

"Alphabet. A B C D E F G."

"Oh, *that* alphabet," said Rose.

"Yeah. Do you know it?"

"No. I didn't go to school but two days and all I learned was my name and teacher's name. That's when I lived in Jacksonville or Houston or wherever I'm from. Don't tell anybody I don't know how to read, Grover."

"I won't."

"You're the onliest person knows outside my sister."

"Where does she live?"

Rose searched the National Geographic map for her sister's whereabouts. "Someplace begins with a dubbya."

"Washington?"

"Maybe that's it. Where the President lives. She works for him."

"Your sister works for the *President of the United States?*"

"Well, I hope to kiss a cow," said Rose with pride at this doubtful accomplishment shining.

Rose hoped to kiss a cow for a lot of things; it was her most favorite expression.

. . . A decent interval should pass, his father said, before he should resume his usual occupations. A great tragedy had just been suffered. Was he completely inpervious to it?

He said, "No, sir, I'm not completely impervious to it. I feel it."

His father turned a lonely, accusing gaze. "You don't act like you do. Where were you off to just now?"

"Nowhere. I was just going fishing with Ellen Grae and Farrell."

"Fishing," his father echoed in cold, incredulous disgust.

So he didn't go.

In midmorning Aunt Marty came with a bushel of peaches from Georgia. She and Rose spent thirty minutes talking about what was to be done with them. Some could be pickled and some could be frozen and some could be eaten now.

They went to his mother's room and opened all the curtains and windows and conferred, in matter-of-fact tones, about what to do with the clothes hanging in the closet, the toilet articles on the dresser, her books. All of it should be put away, said Aunt Marty, and the door to the room should be left open.

"Yu," sighed Rose. "Yu. It ain't good for Mr. Ezell to come home from a hard day's work and come lock hisself up in here with her things."

"No," agreed Aunt Marty. "No, it isn't."

When she left Grover walked with her to her car. She said, "Is that what your father's been doing, Grover? Locking himself up in your mother's room when he comes home from work?"

He looked into her concerned eyes. "He doesn't do it every day, Aunt Marty."

She started the car and he stepped back away from it. She went backward several feet, stopped and then came forward again. She stuck her head out of the car. "You don't do that, do you? Mope in your mother's room?"

"No, Aunt Marty."

She chewed her lips. "I can't talk to him. Neither can Abner. He thinks that we don't sympathize but this isn't true. It's just that it's finished."

He said, "Your front tire looks like it might be a little low, Aunt Marty."

She got out of the car to look. "It might be. I'd better have it checked. Does he talk to you about it, Grover? About your mother? Does he say how he feels?"

"No, Aunt Marty."

Which was a partial lie. Once he *had* talked to him about it, shattering the evening stillness with his anger. Saying, "It is the chief duty of *every* human being to endure life." But not expecting an answer or even understanding.

. . . When he went back inside Rose had him read from the cookbook how to pickle peaches:

"Take one peck of peaches. Pour four quarts of boiling water over them. Drain them. Peel them. Place in each peach five whole cloves minus the heads. Take eight cups of sugar and one quart of mild vinegar and . . . should I keep on reading? There's a lot more. How're you gonna remember it all?"

"You jus' read," replied Rose. "And leave the rememberin' part to me."

After the peaches Rose went to his mother's room and took her clothes from the hangers, folded them in layers of white tissue paper and packed them in the cedar chest beneath the window. She took all the bottles and jars off the dresser and put them in two shoe boxes. The bed had already been stripped, even to the mattress, and the rug removed. Now it was just an empty, airy room filled with afternoon sunlight.

"She liked the air-conditioner," Grover said. "It made her feel better."

Rose gave the gleaming floor a final swipe with her mop and came to the doorway and put her cool palm on the back of his neck. "It had to be done, little shaver. When something's finished you got to let go of it."

They left the door to the room standing wide and went back to the kitchen and drank chocolate milk with blobs of vanilla ice cream. Rose said her feet hurt and took her shoes off. "When you goin' to teach me how to read?" she inquired.

"As soon as you learn the alphabet."

"The alphabet," said Rose. "A B C D E F G."

"That's only part of it."

"It is? What's the rest?"

"H I J K L M N O P."

"Is that all?"

"Q R S T U V. W X Y Z."

"A B C D E F G H I J K L M N O P Q R S T U V W X Y Z," said Rose and cackled with laughter.

He said, "You knew it all the time, didn't you?"

"Well, I hope to kiss a cow," said Rose.

He sat on the front steps and waited for his father to come home. The westering sun was a clear, dry yellow. The wind made the wrought-iron weathercock on top of the garage turn first to the east and then to the west, creaking each time it turned. And all around there was this silent, invisible energy.

A long, serpentine ribbon of pure, rose-colored light appeared on the horizon, stretched endlessly from the skyline to infinity. He thought about his mother.

His father came and he was dusty and brusque. He didn't want to talk to him. "Later," he said and went on into the house.

The long shadows of evening appeared and so did Rose. Her shoes, knotted together by the strings, hung from her neck. "I'm fired," she said. "He didn't like me putting her things away and cleaning up her room so I'm fired."

Grover walked down the road with her, intending to go only as far as the turn but in the end went all the way home with her. To her three stifled rooms and makeshift bath perched on brick stilts within sight and smell of the Thicket garbage dump.

He was invited to admire the clumps of marigolds growing at her door, her calendar pictures tacked in precision array on her walls, her braided rugs, her radio.

"After a while your daddy will be worried about you so you better not stay too long," said Rose. "You hungry?"

"No, ma'am."

"Thirsty?"

"No, ma'am."

"Me neither," sighed Rose. "I ain't nothin' but tired."

They sat on her back stoop where it was cooler and watched the sparks from the fires in the dump erupt. Like frayed topiary figures in some science-fiction garden, a bedspring and an old skeletal car leaned against each other, stark in the wavering light.

Grover said, "He's not a mean man, my father. He just feels so bad since my mother went away. That's what makes him act like he does."

Rose moved closer to him. He smelled her cool, smooth skin and her soap. Her voice was like rippled silk. "I know that, little shaver. Don't worry about it. Don't worry about anything."

"She told me that he was equal. Equal to any situation. By that she meant that he wouldn't go to pieces when the time came. But, oh, Lordy, he feels bad. I do, too."

Rose made little clucking sounds with her mouth.

"Do you know what he told me, Rose? He told me that it is the chief duty of every human being to endure life. Do you believe that, Rose?"

Rose sighed. "I don' know. What's endure mean?"

"Endure means to suffer things out. It means to . . . be patient with things even if you're suffering."

Rose made more clucking sounds. "To be patient with things even if you're suffering. Oh, little shaver, I don't know about that. I sure don't know the answer to that one. I'm sorry."

"Well, that's okay."

The air buzzed suddenly with mosquitoes but a waft of white smoke drove them away.

"That's one good thing about livin' here," observed Rose. "The smoke from the dump keeps the mosquitoes away."

He said, "Rose are you going back?"

"Sure. Who'd look out after you and your daddy if I didn't?"

"When? When are you going back?"

"Tomorrow, maybe. Or maybe tonight. Maybe I'll go back with you when you go. Want me to?"

He said yes and she went back with him.

His father, beneath the reading lamp in the living room, merely looked up and said, "Mrs. McGruder brought a bushel of peaches, Rose. I put them on the back porch."

"More peaches," sighed Rose. "People keep bringing peaches you goin' to have to buy me some more jars."

His father grunted and went back to his paper.

It was a truce but not a truce. On his way to the bathroom Grover noticed that the door to his mother's room was closed again. He opened it and looked in and saw that everything was back the way it had been. To hide its bareness his father had covered the bed with a thick, blue spread and placed two pillows at its head.

Chapter Seven

In this town of Thicket there was only one hill and all of it was owned by one person--a strong, dark-skinned, unmarried woman by the name of Betty Repkin. She had stiff orange hair and a tattoo on her arm.

Betty Repkin was a misanthrope—a hater of mankind. They said that she wasn't this way at first—that when she first came she wanted to be friends and gave a big outdoor party but nobody went. They said she waited for them to come until midnight. Then she took all of the food she had cooked up, put it in her station wagon, carted it down the hill and deposited it in sloppy piles on the steps of the Methodist church. Then she went back home and waited for Sheriff Fudge to come and arrest her but he didn't. The next morning the ladies from the church went and cleaned up the mess and that was the end of it—except that Thicket had made an enemy.

On Betty Repkin's hill there stood a house with a white stone front. A lacy frieze ornamented its top. The grounds surrounding the house abounded in things worthy of attention: a gaudy circus wagon with a picture of a woman swallowing fire painted on its sides, a row of espaliered trees, their branches trained on wires to spread in fan shapes, peacocks that made a terrible racket when awake, a flock of pampered turkeys. When her out-of-town friends came Betty Repkin always killed a couple of these. The people who lived closest to the hill said they could smell them roasting.

Betty Repkin was mean and stingy so nobody liked to work for her but one day Ellen Grae and Farrell and Grover got themselves hauled into doing a job for her. They weren't looking for it; they were just walking around on her hill, on the lower slopes of it, enjoying the coolness, when suddenly, in the deep-piled patch just above them she appeared.

"She's going to tell us to get off her property," warned Ellen Grae. "She doesn't allow people on it un-invited. We should have remembered but it's too late now. She's seen us. Should we run or should we just stand here and get ourselves bawled out? Oh, look, she's waving. She's not mad. Go see what she wants, Grover."

Betty Repkin had a fleshy smile and cold, black eyes. She fixed those eyes on Grover and asked how would he and Ellen Grae and Farrell like to do a little yard work for her. That some of her friends were coming the next day and she wanted her yard to look nice for them. For a good job she'd pay them each fifty cents an hour. "Go and ask your little friends if they'll do it," she said. "I'll wait here."

Farrell and Ellen Grae agreed to it with some grum-blings. Farrell said that fifty cents an hour was starvation wages and Ellen Grae muttered under her breath but they went with Grover and Betty Repkin up to her house and walked around with her letting her show them what she wanted done.

She belittled how much of it there was. She said, "Aw come on now. Don't show me them long faces. They ain't enough work here to fill up a gnat's eye. If you organize it right it won't take you hardly no more'n an hour. Lookit the good tools you got to work with. This here one with the little claw is a weed puller. See how easy the lawn mower goes. Just a little twist of the handle like this and it fires right up. You don't have to push it. All you got to do is guide it. Like this. See?"

Before they got down to the business of working she was friendly and nice. Farrell had to use the bathroom and she let him enter the house through the side door. To relieve their thirst, which she said she knew would come, she brought out a bucket of ice water and three jelly glasses. She gave them each a rag to wipe sweat with. She gave them permission to splash themselves with the hose when they got too hot. She said she had to go inside and cook food for the coming day but if they needed anything just to give a holler.

Farrell made himself a sultan's turban out of his rag and skipped around in a circle waiting for somebody to tell him what to do. He described Betty Repkin's bathroom—blue tub, blue sink, blue toilet paper, some false teeth soaking in a jar. All not very clean.

Ellen Grae said, "Farrell, who cares? I certainly don't. How did we get into this anyway? I swear, Grover, you do have the strangest notions sometimes. Well, the sooner we get started the quicker we'll get done. You'd better look at your watch, Grover, and see what time it is. We're getting paid by the hour, don't forget."

It was exactly ten o'clock. The heat bearing down
upon them was savage. They breathed parched air and
huffed and puffed. Vertical stripes, caused by the sweat
cutting down through the dust, appeared on their
faces.

By mistake Farrell clawed six lilies out of the ground
and furiously chopped them to bits. He said he thought
they were dandelions. There wasn't any use in trying to
set them back in their holes and pretend like they were
still alive. Farrell wouldn't so Grover gathered up the
pieces and took them to the back door and told Betty
Repkin what had happened and after a long look she
said, "Well, that's pretty stupid. Anybody can't tell a
lily from a dandelion can't be very bright. What's your
name? I forgot to ask you."

He told her that his name was Grover Ezell and her
eyes widened and she stared at him but then she said,
"Well, all right. Get on back to work. We'll talk about
the lilies later."

Farrell said that he didn't care if Betty Repkin's lawn
never got done, that *she* was stupid for putting lilies
where dandelions should be and that he wasn't going to
work any more. He sat down in a patch of shade and
watched Ellen Grae and Grover.

With a cutter that needed sharpening Ellen Grae
hacked at the grass around the flower beds and cussed
and drank more than her share of the ice water.

The lawn mower wasn't as easy to start as Betty
Repkin had demonstrated but once Grover got it going
it did a fair job of shearing.

A turkey wandered up, stuck his head through a
bristle of hedge and watched.

"He's probably the daddy to all those other dumb

turkeys wandering around out there," observed Ellen Grae. "Look at him, the way he struts. Look how conceited he is."

"He'd look good in a roasting pan," murmured Farrell and with flailed hands and bulging eyes showed the turkey the first step toward this end.

Alarm swept across the turkey's face. He jerked his head free of the hedge, lifted his spindly legs and tore out across the clipped lawn. His wild screams rent the air.

It brought Betty Repkin to the back door. She had flour on her face and her stiff, orange hair was standing straight up. "What's going on out here?" she cried. "What'd you do to my bird? You crazy? Let him alone! You'll turn his liver sour!"

Grover had to bear the brunt of this. Ellen Grae had melted into a tree trunk and Farrell into the dark, loamy earth beneath a cluster of cherry laurel bushes.

Still flapping and squawking the turkey reached a rise in the land, hesitated, tried to pump his pot-bellied body into the air, failed, and with a final shriek staggered out of view.

"Stupid!" screeched Betty Repkin. "You stupid boy! What's the matter with you? You crazy? What'd you do to my bird to make him run like that? You hit him? Throw a rock at him?"

"No, ma'am," Grover hollered. "I didn't hit him or throw any rock at him. Farrell just said how good he'd look in a roasting pan and it scared him, I reckon. We didn't know he could understand English!"

Betty Repkin's square legs carried her body out of her doorway, down the steps, and across the freshly manicured turf. She bounced. Her shapeless mouth quivered. "Smart kid," she hissed. "You talk too smart for your size, boy. You think smart?"

"No, ma'am, I don't think smart. I don't know what . . . listen, Mrs. Repkin, we didn't hurt your old turkey. It was just a joke. All Farrell . . . all we said to him was how good he'd look in a roasting pan. That's all, I swear it. We didn't know he'd understand us. We didn't hurt your turkey. Maybe there's something else wrong with him, causing him to carry on like that. Maybe he's got an allergy or fleas."

The black eyes had thunderstorms in them. Betty Repkin's hand went to her chin and stroked. "Smart kid," she said, ladling the words out of her mouth in little dips. "You're just like everybody else in this town. Smart with the words but no brains. I know you; I place you now. You're the kid whose mother blew her brains out."

The shadows beneath the cherry laurel were navy blue. They stirred and Farrell's dirt-streaked face looked out.

The smell from the warm, barbered grass rose to Grover's nostrils in great, labored waves.

Betty Repkin didn't look at Farrell. She fastened her eyes on Grover's forehead and in a toughly timbered voice, spitefully and triumphantly said, "I went to her funeral. Nobody invited me but I went anyway. The undertaker did a good job layin' her out. You couldn't even tell she had shot herself, the way they had her face patched up. They left some cotton in her nose though. I saw her at the funeral home."

Ellen Grae came out from behind her tree and walked toward Betty Repkin and Grover. When she reached the cherry laurel she said, "Come out, Farrell. We've got trouble."

They came and flanked him.

Betty Repkin ignored them. She smiled at Grover. "Well, boy, ain't you going to say anything? Where's all your smart talk now?"

Farrell thrust his stomach and chin out. He said, "You're an ugly old varmint and your home is dirty. No wonder nobody likes you."

Betty Repkin's smile enveloped Grover, smothered him. "Suicide is a coward's way," she said. "And it's you and your dad'll pay for it a little bit, too, huh? *Then* we'll see how smart you talk."

Ellen Grae loudly popped her gum, gave a hitch to her pants and gazed at Betty Repkin. "I spit on you and all your dreams," she said.

Betty Repkin said, "Get off my property."

Farrell said, "We're going. But you owe us for two hours. You going to pay us?"

Grover said, "Oh, come on, let's go." And they left without picking up the tools—without getting paid.

Betty Repkin screamed something at them but they didn't look back. On the way down the hill they passed the turkey that had caused all the trouble. He shook his red wattle and preened his bronze feathers and leered.

"Smart bird," muttered Farrell. "I oughta run my fist down his throat and turn him wrong side out. *That'd* fix that old Betty Repkin's sweet patootie." His eyes filled suddenly with glittering tears. He stepped closer to Grover and made an intense effort to match steps.

With her gum Ellen Grae blew a glossy, pink bubble. She wiped her soiled hands on her pants and after a moment of consideration reached and grasped Grover's wrist with one of them. She said, "Go ahead and shake if you have to, Grover. It's nothing to be ashamed of. I always shake when I'm mad."

They went down the hill.

In Thicket the summer dawns come the color of silver. Everything is soaked with night moisture. Underfoot the pathways are cool. Above the town Betty Repkin's hill slumbers in swirls of gray mist.

The mist was thick and clammy, but Farrell said they'd better be glad for it, that it would hide them. "Let's just find that old bird," he whispered. "That's what we came out here for so let's hurry up and do it."

From the branches of an ancient oak two peacocks with their brilliant plumage drooping, sleepily watched them pass. Ellen Grae stared up at them. She said, "Grover, if we can't find the turkey we could settle for one of those. It'd pain Betty Repkin just as bad. Everybody says she's crazy about her peacocks. Hey, what time do turkeys get up anyway? Maybe she keeps them locked up at night. You reckon?"

"No, Ellen Grae."

"You don't know that. You're just guessing. What if she does?"

"She doesn't keep them locked up at night, Ellen Grae. They're out here wandering around someplace. Turkeys are like chickens. They get up at daylight."

"There's a whole flock of them," said Ellen Grae. "How are you going to recognize the one you're looking for?"

"I'll recognize him, don't worry."

Ellen brushed drops of moisture from her hair and forehead. "Grover, I know how you feel."

"That's good. I'm glad somebody does."

"She shouldn't have said that about your mother."

"That's right; she shouldn't have."

"Nobody likes her. Everybody wishes she'd leave. She's real low-down. Grover?"

"What?"

"You sure you want to do this?"

"I'm positive. Shut up, Ellen Grae. Just shut up."

Beneath their feet the forest duff was slick and wet. Far above them, veiled in misty gloom, Betty Repkin's house loomed in silent, frozen fantasy.

"She's mean," whispered Farrell. "And ugly. The ugliest human I ever saw."

Ellen Grae sighed and shifted the wool blanket she had brought from home.

With his sharpened hatchet Grover lopped a branch.

Now the mists were lifting and the last traces of darkness were dissolving into nothingness. In the high grasses living things scuttled and squeaked.

They left the trees and came to a slight mound in the land and climbed it and went down the other side and there in the clearing saw their quarry wobbling around on his stilt legs. He had his head down, was vigorously pecking at something in the earth but at some sound they made he jerked erect, spread his tail feathers, and furtively looked around in their direction. Behind him there was a spread of low field fence and he turned and looked at that, too, wary speculation in his red eyes.

"He knows," whispered Farrell. "Look at him, Grover. He knows."

Grover said, "Yeah. Don't talk. Throw him some bread."

Farrell took two slices of bread from the inside of his

shirt and began breaking them into small bits. The turkey watched him and made a funny, garbling sound in his throat.

A resin-scented wind stirred the grasses near the fence. It tasted sour. Something in Grover's stomach dribbled.

Beside him Ellen Grae was carefully unfolding the blanket. Her breath was coming and going from her mouth in little puffed jerks. She said, "Grover?"

"What?"

"You're sure this is what you want to do, huh?"

"Yes, I'm sure. Start moving around toward the fence and have the blanket ready. What's the matter?"

"Nothing, Grover."

"You want to back out? If you do, go ahead. I didn't force you to come out here with me. You said you wanted to."

"I know I did. I don't want to back out, Grover."

"Then shut up talking and don't look at me like that. Start working your way around toward the fence and have the blanket ready. As soon as he turns his back on me I'm going to rush him. If we can just get him up against the fence we can slap the blanket over him."

Into Ellen Gray's face there came a curious mingled look—of reproach and stilled anger and unwilling compassion. But she sidled over to the fence and, holding the blanket carelessly so that the turkey wouldn't suspect what they were trying to do, leaned against it. She hummed a little tune.

The turkey swiveled around and looked at her and the feathers on his neck rippled.

Grover took some cautious steps that put him behind the turkey. The bird jerked around for a hard look.

Grover forced a smile. The turkey shook his wattle and made more sounds in his throat.

Farrell edged around until he was standing beside Ellen Grae. Gently he flicked two bits of bread toward the turkey. They landed within an inch of him and he jerked back, bristling with suspicion.

Leaning against the fence, Ellen Grae sighed.

The dribbling in Grover's stomach had increased. His heart was thrashing and there was sweat in the small of his back. The turkey twisted his head around and looked at him beseechingly. Though only one of his eyes was visible to him, it seemed to Grover that he was looking straight at him and horribly; all in the breadth of one second, he thought he detected intelligence and hurt and humiliation in the red, fearful eye and the dribbling in him became a cold stream. But then as quickly as it had come this moment of near-pity was drowned in a rushing surge of other stronger feelings.

To Farrell he said, "Throw him another piece of bread," and Farrell tore it from the slice in his hand and flung it out and the turkey swung around and gave it his greedy attention, moving eagerly toward it.

Grover moved, too. He gave a couple of big, quick leaps, like a kangaroo and landed squarely on top of him.

"The blanket!" he screamed to Ellen Grae, holding on with desperate strength to the frightened, flapping, squawking bird. "Throw the blanket over him!"

He kicked and struggled and emitted terrible, anguished cries but they got the blanket over him and knotted it and carried him back into the trees where it was cooler and darker. There was a fallen log there and they got him up on it. He writhed and threshed and

groaned and screamed but Grover chopped his head off. It wasn't a good, clean kill. Blood spurted from the wound in his throat but still he clawed the air and struggled for his life.

Somewhere in all of this Ellen Grae tried to stop Grover. She grabbed his arm and shook him and said, "Grover, stop! It won't make anything better! It won't change anything!"

"Shut up!" he said. And pushed her away.

Farrell's face and hands and the front of his shirt were flecked with blood and his face was the color of old concrete. He kept swallowing. He avoided looking at Grover. "Is it dead?" he whispered. "Is it dead?"

Ellen Grae had her lower lip in her teeth. There was red froth in her hair and on her nose and cheeks. There were furious tears in her eyes. She said, "Get it over with! Just get it over with!"

The liquid in his stomach erupted and boiled up . . . he swallowed it, took a tighter grip on the squirming turkey and brought his hatchet down again on the scrawny neck and this time it separated from the rest of him. His head, the eyes horribly bulging, fell to the ground and his body jerked out of the hands that held it and flew up into the air and came down again and started dancing around. But after a minute or two it gave a big, convulsive shudder, which sent some more blood spraying, collapsed, and was finally dead.

They left it there for Betty Repkin to find.

On the way back down the hill Ellen Grae didn't speak to Grover nor did Farrell.

Chapter Eight

Grover had never known his father to be religious—had never seen him read the Bible or heard him speak of God. Had never heard him say that he loved or hated religion or feared it. But now in this season of affliction he saw his father seek its usefulness—the hope it might create—the comfort its influence might bring.

In the dimness of his mother's room Grover saw his father kneeling and knew that he was trying to pray and he wondered at his father's expression which contained neither trust nor expectancy nor humility—only helplessness. And he thought: He's not doing it right. He should get Reverend Vance to show him how.

But he couldn't say this to his father.

On Sundays they now went to church and sat in a pew with Uncle Ab and Aunt Marty and listened to the reasonable sermons. Reverend Vance had a pure voice; the way he spoke from his pulpit was pure. He didn't scream and wave his arms and threaten people. He spoke of the immense power of God over mankind in an orderly way. He had a quiet, classroom manner.

Reverend Vance's sermons did not seem to have an improving effect on Grover's father.

Grover asked Rose if they made *her* feel any better and with a look she said, "Not much. He sings mighty purty though. His singin' makes me feel like I could sprout wings and fly right out the window. But his talkin' and prayin' kind of rankles me. It takes him so long to get to what he's asking for. *My* prayin' only takes *me* a second."

"You say prayers?"

"Yu, yu. You want this banana? It broke off from the rest."

He accepted the banana. "What do you say when you pray?"

"Oh, nothin' fancy. 'Now I lay me down to sleep, I pray the Lord my soul to keep. If I should die before I wake, I pray the Lord my soul to take.' "

"Do you think He will?"

"Take my soul? Well, I hope to kiss a cow. The way I got it figured out He's going to take everybody's."

"Everybody's?"

"Everybody's."

"And then what?"

Rose took a meaty soup bone from the refrigerator and plopped it into a pot of simmering water. "Well, then when we all get where we're goin' there'll be some changes made."

"What kind of changes?"

"Oh," replied Rose with a blithe air, "the people who've cheated and robbed and lied and murdered will catch it then. They'll have to grub and slave from sunup to sundown. They'll have to do all the work. Us people who've been good will get to lie around and eat chocolates all day long." She touched the shaggy, yellow blossom in her hair. "But why we talkin' like this, little shaver? Today my soul's not goin' anywhere and neither is yours. Read me some out of the paper."

"Okay. What part?"

"I don't care. Is there anything in it about the President?"

"No, I don't see anything."

"They don't write enough about him," said Rose and tossed an onion into the soup pot.

Rose liked things in an uproar: the soup bubbling, the iron hissing, big, glistening soap bubbles floating out all the doors and windows. Mornings with her were fierce.

He went out and got his bicycle out of the garage and rode it across town. He saw a man trying to teach a woman how to drive. As they careened past him he got a glimpse of their faces; hers was serene, his was terrified. At the end of the street she jerked to a stop and he got out and sat on the curb.

A small boy in an open-faced yard stopped Grover and showed him a pile of latticed sticks laid over a hole. "It's a layroo to catch meddlers with," he whispered.

"What's a layroo?"

"This is," he cooed. "I made it up. When it gets dark a meddler will come along and step in it and break his leg. Won't that be funny?"

Sprinklers laid wings of water over Mrs. Merriweather's plant nursery.

Reverend Vance was in his driveway working on the engine of his car. Prying and peering he said, "It keeps stalling on me. I think there's water in the battery although for the life of me I can't figure out how it got there. Rats. I need a smaller wrench. Do you see one over there, Grover? In that box there?"

Grover looked in the box and found a smaller wrench and handed it to Reverend Vance. "But the battery is supposed to have water in it, sir."

Reverend Vance raised his head and looked at him. "Are you sure?"

"Yes, sir. If car batteries didn't have water in them they wouldn't charge."

Reverend Vance stared at the battery and made vague motions with the wrench. "Well, this is a little out of my line."

"Yes, sir, but it's good to know about these things. This here is a wet cell battery. That's why it has to have water in it. You know flashlights?"

"Yes, I know flashlights."

"Flashlights have dry cell batteries in them but cars have wet cell batteries. You going to leave those wires hanging loose like that? If you do your car won't start."

Reverend Vance put the wires back where they belonged, gathered up his tools and invited Grover to go inside with him. He had a new possession—an antique organ, heavy and brown and all-walnut with an ornate mirror above the music rack. He flicked a switch and something inside the box whirred. "That noise you hear is from the vacuum cleaner," he explained. "It's under the house. Sheriff Fudge hooked it up to the organ for me so I wouldn't have to pump when I wanted to play. You want to try it? It's easy."

"No, sir, I don't know anything about playing an organ. I don't know one note from another."

Reverend Vance's long, thin fingers flowed over the

keys and an array of triumphant Christians blew trumpets and sang.

After the music they went out into the back yard and looked at four mole holes and four mounds of freshly dug earth. "I don't like to kill the little animals," said Reverend Vance. "But I'm going to have to do something. They're chewing up my whole lawn."

Grover said, "My mother used to feed them garlic. I never asked her why but come to think of it maybe it just makes them sick enough to want to go someplace else. I'm sure it wouldn't kill them. My mother liked animals, too. Anyway, why don't you try it?"

They fed the mole holes a whole box of garlic, poking the cloves way down with a stick. They sat on the steps and waited for results. There was wind in the eucalyptus trees and a warm droning in the flower borders.

Grover said, "I liked your sermon yesterday. It made good sense."

Reverend Vance turned his large, brilliant eyes. "Thank you, Grover. I kind of liked it myself."

"Friends are the best property of all, just like you said. And I think people *should* divide their troubles and grief with them. That way it makes the person you're dividing them with feel like he's doing something to help somebody and it makes you feel better because you've got rid of part of it."

"Exactly," agreed Reverend Vance.

"But some people don't want friends. They don't want to divide their troubles and grief with anybody else."

"That's true."

"If you knew somebody like that—somebody that was important to you—what would you do?"

Reverend Vance looked out across the yard at the mole holes and the piles of dirt. "I'd wait," he said. "Grief has to be digested. Sometimes when it's fresh, offers to be friends and share only irritate."

A shag of grass near the entrance to one of the mole holes quivered. A polished cone containing a tree snail left a trail of slime as it rippled from one green blade to another.

Grover asked a question: "Reverend Vance, do you think it's the chief duty of every human being to endure life even when they know they're sick and going to die?"

The brilliant eyes blinked and the expression in the delicate face shifted. Reverend Vance turned and stared at the mole holes. In the sunshine his hair was yellow and smooth, like a baby's. The skin on the back of his neck was smooth, too, and very fair. He clasped his hands around his knees. He seemed to be struggling to find an answer but none came and, watching him search for uncertain words, Grover knew that he had put the minister in a bad spot and felt sorry for him and didn't want his answer after all.

Grover said, "My father says it is. He says that but I don't think he really means it. I think he just says it because it hasn't been too long since my mother . . . went away and he's lonesome. I'm lonesome, too, but we're different. My father and I are different."

"Yes," murmured Reverend Vance.

"I'm tough. That's because I've got more Cornett in me than Ezell. My mother was a Cornett before she married my father. Us Cornetts don't howl about things. There's no sense in howling; it doesn't do a bit of good. When something bad happens to you, like your mother dying, you've got to go it alone, the way I've got it figured out. You've got to use your gumption and common sense."

"Yes, of course," said Reverend Vance, still with his face and back turned.

Grover said, "I wish I could figure out what being dead is and I wish I could get it settled in my mind where people go when they die. That's the question I *really* came over here to ask you. Not that other one."

The beautiful, delicate face turned. The eyes and the mouth relaxed and smiled. Came the minister's soft, pure answer, word for word, from Corinthians II, Chapter five, verse 1: "For we know that if our earthly house of this tabernacle were dissolved, we have a building of God, an house not made with hands, eternal in the heavens."

A mole with his mouth full of garlic emerged from one of the holes. He didn't look the least bit sick.

He's a good and honorable man, thought Grover. Everybody in Thicket agrees to that. He inspires other people to be good and honorable themselves. But I don't know if he knows the answers to everything. He can't say that it's the chief duty of every human being to endure life even when they're sick and know they're going to die. He can't say that because he's never been that way.

Chapter Nine

There was this stretch of days during which it seemed to him that he moved in one direction and everybody else moved in another.

He had a falling out with Ellen Grae and Farrell. At the crack of dawn one morning they sneaked down to the river without him and painted his boat and everything in it and on it a thick cherry red. At a distance it didn't look too bad but up close it was one horrendous mess.

"How much thinner did you use?" he asked.

They looked at him. "Thinner? Thinner? We didn't use any thinner. What's thinner?"

"Thinner is what makes paint dry. This stuff is never going to. You see how sticky it is? That's the way it'll be this time next month because you didn't use any thinner. What a mess."

Ellen Grae thrust her chin out. "It'll dry if you'll just get off of it. If you'll just give it a chance. Maybe we *should* tow it up to where the sun can get to it though.

You're tracking it up, Grover. What are you looking for?"

"Nothing, Ellen Grae. I'm just looking. For crying in public, what a mess! Oh, for crying in public, here's my new bug all smeared up! Which of you brains did this?"

Farrell moved around to where he was in back of Ellen Grae. "I did," he admitted. "I guess I kind of got carried away."

"It's ruined! Everything is. If this isn't one heck of a mess I never saw one. You know what you two are? Numbskulls. Nobody but a numbskull would pull a trick like this! Why'd you do it? Did anybody ask you to? You like to paint so much why don't you go pick on some of your own stuff? Oh, what a mess! Everything is ruined. I swear, Ellen Grae. I know you're a girl and all but haven't you got *any* sense?"

Farrell stuck his head out from behind Ellen Grae and said, "Now, lambie, you shouldn't talk to Ellen Grae like that."

He said, "You shut up, you little pest. You little . . . Yankee."

Ellen Grae drew Farrell out and put her arm around him. "Ingrate," she said. "You're nothing but an ingrate, Grover Ezell. Farrell and I have been down here slaving like dogs since five o'clock this morning and this is the thanks we get for it. You should be ashamed of yourself."

"Ingrate," echoed Farrell, blinking his eyes. "You'll be sorry you talked to us like that."

"Crab," said Ellen Grae. "You've turned into an old dried-up crab, Grover. You don't *want* your friends to share your problems with you. You want to hog them all to yourself and be miserable. So go and be miserable. Farrell and I don't care. We don't care a smidgen. All we were trying to do was make you feel better about things but you don't want to feel better. You're selfish and hateful, Grover."

Farrell hugged himself and with love and respect shining through he gazed at Ellen Grae.

Ellen Grae smiled at him and reached out and took his hand. They turned and ran off through the trees, leaving Grover standing there in the sticky, smelly boat.

They aren't my friends any more, he thought, and a bitter liquid burned in his mouth and throat. But then he thought. Aw, for crying in public, what's wrong with you? It's not them that's wrong. It's you. And he wanted to run after them and tell them that he was sorry but something—pride, maybe—kept him from it.

On Wednesday evening he went with Aunt Marty and Uncle Ab and Rose to prayer meeting. His father refused an invitation to go along. They left him sitting beside his darkened lamp.

At the door Grover looked back at his father and his heart quickened with pity but he couldn't say anything. He went on.

It seemed to him then that he felt sorry for everybody, even people who didn't need sympathy: Miss Hasty and Miss Rogers and Tony, the gravedigger, and Sheriff Fudge and Aunt Marty and Uncle Ab and Ramona Gookizen—even Mrs. Merriweather who was deaf as a post. He didn't think Mrs. Merriweather minded being deaf. She always snoozed during church and prayer meetings. Still, he was sorry for her. He was even sorry for Betty Repkin. He wished that he hadn't killed her turkey.

It seemed to him then that there was something missing in people. Most of all he noticed this in his father. There was something in him that was missing. He would look at his father and he would say to himself, Oh, my father, I wish that I could help you.

There was something missing in himself, too.

Rose said she'd like to have a mess of good, freshwater catfish to make a stew out of and asked when could he go down to the river and catch her some.

He said, "Never. I hate catfish stew."

"Seems to me," observed Rose, "like you hate a lot of things lately. I've been keeping track. In the last three days you know how many things you've told me you hated?"

"No. Quit jawing at me."

Rose took a paper bag of black-eyed peas from the refrigerator and settled herself at the table to shell them. She said, "I'm not jawin' at you, honey. I'm jus' trying to find out what it is that's frettin' you so. You sure you don't want to tell me? I'll betcha I could help. Come on, tell me."

"There isn't anything to tell. I've told you that a hundred times. Where'd all these flowers come from?"

Making quick decisions on which pods to shell and which to snap Rose's hands moved from the bag to the colander and from the colander to the bag. "The florist brought 'em. They're to take to your mama's grave. Your daddy'll be home in a little bit. Said for me to tell you to be ready. Wants you to go to the cemetery with

him. You better go change your clothes. You sure can't
go like that."

The flowered stalks, stood upright in a pail of water
on the drainboard, didn't have any smell to them so it
couldn't have been them which gave him a headache.
But something did and there was this queer anxiety in
his stomach.

His father came home, shaved again, changed his
shirt, wrapped the flowers in waxed paper and carried
them out to the car.

Rose wanted them to eat first but with a wintry look
his father said, "No. Later."

They didn't talk during the drive to the cemetery. It
seemed to Grover like they never had. He tried to remember when they had last talked but nothing came to
his mind except, small, strained fragments.

The outskirting streets of Thicket lay peaceful in the
noon heat. On the far eastern horizon a bank of low,
dark clouds boiled.

His father drove faster than he usually did. Grover
glanced at his set profile and something inside him
began to work.

Around Friendship cemetery there was a thick, gray
wall with squared, spaced openings near its top and in
one of these squares there was a dove which cooed the
whole time they were there. *Coo. Coo. Coo. Coo.*

The grass around and between the plots was bril-
liantly green. Near a white, wooden cross a woman
prayed. They went past her and she didn't look up. She
was old.

They found his mother's grave. There was a carved
piece of pink marble with her name, date of birth, and
date of death inscribed on it in flowed letters and

::110::

Grover said how pretty it was but his father only nodded, unable to speak. He knelt and awkwardly placed the flowers.

"They might blow away," Grover said. "It's going to rain."

His father acted like he hadn't heard. Still kneeling, he put his palms down into the soft, green turf and began kneading it.

"She isn't here," Grover said, trying to share his belief.

His father turned grief-stricken eyes but they didn't see.

The dove's cooing was very sweet and very tender. *Coo. Coo. Coo. Coo.*

"She would have changed," Grover said, speaking a new knowledge. "I've seen animals who've been sick for a long time and they always do. She would have, too. That's why she did it. She would have changed and she didn't want us to see it. Shouldn't we go home now? It's going to rain."

His father reached and laid one hand on the pink marker. "Ahhhhh," he said. "Ahhhhhhhh. How can anybody say this is fair? She didn't have to go. She could have waited." He balled his fist and brought it against his mouth. The tears in his eyes were enormous. He squeezed his lids together and the tears rolled out of his eyes and splashed down on his cheeks. "Ahhhh-hhhh," he whispered. "Ahhhhhhhh."

Why, it's himself he's sorry for, Grover thought. Not her. He's sorry for himself because he's alone now except for me.

And then he thought, He's not even trying. He knows there isn't any way out of it but he isn't even trying. He doesn't *want* his tears wiped away like it says in Isaiah.

And then he thought, She said he was equal to any situation. This is what she was talking about that day. But if she could see him now she'd know he wasn't equal to this. Should I try to talk to him? It's so hard to know what to say and he doesn't really want me here. Oh, I don't feel good either but people only sympathize up to a point; then you have to go it alone. Then you have to depend on your own gumption and common sense.

"Coo," crooned the dove. "Coo. Coo."

Thunder muttered in the distance.

"Ahhhhhhhh," whispered his father and stroked the pink marker. "Ahhhhhhhh."

Grover said, "Shouldn't we go now? It's going to rain."

"You don't understand," said his father in curious anger. "How could you? You were only her son."

Again the thunder muttered.

Well, he thought, I can't think about it any more. The only thing to do is go on like I'm going and not howl about it. I've got more Cornett in me than Ezell and I've never howled about things. My mother said so. I'm not going to think about this any more. Or worry about what death is. Maybe death is time or space and we're all a part of it. That makes sense. But I'm not going to think about it any more. I'm just going to go on like I'm going and not howl about things and after a while things'll ease up. They will.

And thinking like that, standing there beside his father in the cemetery with the dove cooing and a flurry of wild rain beginning, his mind turned a corner.

Chapter Ten

There was this day of days during which everything fell into place. Farrell and Ellen Grae were a part of it. They came huffing down the road about six thirty in the morning, whooping and hollering like they owned the whole country. Along the way they had picked up Rose. She had her shoes tied together and slung around her neck by the strings and wore a halo of red hibiscus blossoms.

Farrell said he'd been sick. Grover asked him what from and he blinked his rain-colored eyes and said, "From boiled peanuts, that's what from. Ellen Grae and I cooked up five pounds and I ate 'em all except one little handful. I never want to see another boiled peanut as long as I live. I swolled up out to here. I thought I was going to bust. I thought I was going to need an operation. If I hadn't been so healthy otherwise I might have."

Ellen Grae had on a white canvas hat decorated with brightly colored fisherman's flies. Her hair was pushed back out of sight. She gave a hitch to her pants and

said, "Grover, I hope you've had breakfast. If you
haven't, just grab something out of the refrigerator and
let's go. We're late already."

He and Ellen Grae had been friends for a long time
so he knew what she was talking about without asking.
He ran back into the house for his tackle box. Rose
came after him and hurled some cold fried chicken and
some leftover chocolate cake into a bag for them to take
along.

"Don't you want to go with us?" he asked.

Rose reached up and with her finger waggled one of
her blossoms. "Sure. But I can't. Your daddy'll be home
for lunch today. You goin' to bring me some catfish?"

"I reckon I will. See my new bug? I made it. Boy, you
oughta see how excited the fish get when they see this
old bug skimming through the water. They get so
worked up they almost climb up into the boat with me.
I have to fight 'em off."

Rose cackled with laughter. She walked to the door
with him. "Be sure and eat."

"Yes'm."

"Watch out for snakes."

"Yes'm."

"And don't forget where you live."

"Haw. That'll be the last thing I forget."

Rose pushed open the screen door and stepped out
on the porch with him. Her dress sparkled with starch.
She laid a cool hand on the back of his neck and said,
"Well, what're you waitin' for?"

"Nothing. I'm going. Rose?"

"What, little shaver?"

"Does my father talk to you?"

She took her hand away and put it in her pocket. She

moved away from him, went to the porch railing. She
was beautiful. She said, "Sometimes he do. Sometimes
he don't. Don't worry about your daddy no more,
Grover. You can't help him. You already found that out,
I think. Jus' you go on and have a good time. Don' forget you promised me some catfish. I expect at least
three nice, fat ones, hear?"

Love for Rose swelled up in him but he didn't let her
see it. It would have embarrassed her.

On the way down to the river Ellen Grae tried to
start one of her long, drawnout stories but he and Farrell sidetracked her. It was about Mexico. She said that
the dry fields, so brown and wrinkled, reminded her of
Mexico.

"What Mexico?" asked Farrell, hugging himself and
skipping around.

"Mexico," replied Ellen Grae. "You know. South of
the border. The land of the sombrero and the elegant
cockroaches."

Grover said, "Ellen Grae, cockroaches aren't elegant.
Don't breathe so hard. It's bad for your lungs."

"I'm not breathing hard, Grover. I'm just breathing.
I've got to have air. Where was I? Oh, yes. Well, as I
was—"

"Is the Thermos jug too heavy for you?"

"No, it's light as a feather. There's only about five
pounds of ice in it. How about the lunch? Rose didn't
put anything heavy in it, did she?"

They exchanged burdens.

"As I was saying," said Ellen Grae with a determined
look. "This land reminds me of Mexico. Jeff and I were
down there one time and—"

"Have a lemon drop," said Farrell and thrust a bag at

her. She accepted one and he danced away hugging himself and chortling.

"You can tell us about Mexico later," Grover said. "Right now you'd better save your energy."

With savage efficiency the sun bore down upon them. They breathed dust and sweated.

They reached the bank of the river and a draft of cool, fresh air rushed up to meet them. Two crusty turtles on their way to take baths looked at them and changed their minds.

The boat had been repainted. Now it was a correct, nautical gray. Ellen Grae and Farrell grinned at Grover.

They slid down the bank and climbed into the boat. Something off their stern cautiously splashed.

Farrell sat down on the boat's center cross seat, crunched lemon drops, and awaited developments. Ellen Grae untied the boat's stern line and they drifted out to the center of the river.

Grover stood up and surveyed their surroundings. "We'll try it here for a while, Ellen Grae."

She flopped her legs over the side of the boat and popped her gum. "Aye, aye, Captain. Your servant, sir."

He stowed his oar and broke out his fishing gear. "Ellen Grae, you aren't ever going to be anybody's servant and you know it. How about just reaching down there in the bucket and fishing me out a fat worm. Good thing you and Farrell remembered to bring bait; I clean forgot it."

Ellen Grae took the lid off the bait bucket, reached down into its wriggling depths and fished out a fat worm and flicked it at him. "Your servant, sir."

He attached the worm to his hook and lowered his weighted line over the side of the boat. It sank beneath the placid surface of the water. He leaned back and tilted his face to the sun. "If you ever *was* to be anybody's servant they'd be sorry, is all I've got to say."

Ellen Grae popped her gum. "Pshaw, man, belay that kind of talk. Between it and your scowling countenance I find myself sorely vexed and put upon. Haul in your catch, you lazy lunk! Can you not see it dangling there from yonder hook?"

He hauled in his catch, a sparkling, silver minnow. Farrell stood up and walked over and looked into its bereft eyes. "Hog," he said. "That worm was almost as big as you."

Grover said, "Farrell, if you want to fish I'll hook up a line for you. Or you can use my new bug if you want."

Farrell hugged himself. "Maybe later I'll do it, lambie. You know something, Grover?"

"What, Farrell?"

"You and Ellen Grae are the best friends a guy ever had," said Farrell. He popped another lemon drop into his mouth and returned to his seat.

Grover looked at Ellen Grae. "Aren't you going to do any fishing, Ellen Grae?"

Her smile contained a distant dream. "No, Captain, I prefer to do aught today. I am plagued with the vapors. A pox upon civilization. With your permission, sir, I'll just lie here and try to forget it. Wouldn't it be nice if we could just stay out here forever? Grow our own manioc and—"

"Our own what?"

"Manioc. That's where tapioca comes from. It grows—"

"I don't like tapioca."

"If we lived here and could never get to town you'd have to learn to like it. Anyway, as I was saying, wouldn't it be nice if we could just live out here forever and grow our own manioc and maize? Think of all this fecund earth and savanna could provide. Don't suck your cheeks like that, Grover. It makes you look like your shrinking."

He stopped sucking his cheeks. "What would there be to eat besides tapioca and maize? If that was all we ever had to put in our stomachs we'd probably get scurvy."

"No, we wouldn't. Have you ever seen an ichthyo-phagist with scurvy?"

Farrell's eyelids were drooping. He laid down on the crossboard.

Grover's stomach was itching. He put a hand inside his shirt and scratched it. "An ichthyophagist?"

"Yes. That's a fisheater. Have you ever seen one with scurvy?"

"No."

"Of course not. They're the healthiest people alive. A dentist told me that one time. He wanted to know why my teeth were so good and strong and I told him that I was an ichthyophagist and he said that was the reason. He said he'd never seen healthier teeth and gums than mine."

"If they were so healthy what were you doing in his office?"

"I beg your pardon?"

"Why'd you have to go to a dentist if your teeth and gums were so healthy?"

"Oh. Well, I don't remember that part. Probably I was just there waiting for either Grace or Jeff. They're always running to dentists to get their teeth pulled or filled or cleaned. That's another part of civilization that repels me. Dentists. Wouldn't it be nice if we could just live out here and never have to go to one?"

"Yeah," he agreed. "But before we get through with this conversation I want to tell you that scurvy comes from not eating enough things with Vitamin C in them. Things like citrus fruits and tomatoes and green peppers and cabbage. In the olden days sailors always came down with scurvy when they went on long voyages because they didn't take along any fresh fruits or vegetables. Mostly all they ate was fish."

Tired of waiting for them to leave and wanting their baths the two turtles again appeared on the bank of the river and plodded down to the water's edge.

Grover said, "Some people eat turtles but I think we'd better let 'em alone. In the water they've got a mean bite."

"Aye, Captain," agreed Ellen Grae.

Farrell was asleep. He was gently snoring. The bag of lemon drops fell from his relaxed hand. His sprawled legs twitched.

The two turtles were enjoying their baths. The gently licking river current breathed on the sides of the boat. Farrell laughed in his sleep. Ellen Grae and Grover woke him and paddled to shore.

Farrell said he was thirsty and each of them had a swig from the Thermos jug. Then they beached the boat and got out of it and looked around. There were some strange dried animal tracks and Farrell and Grover went over and knelt to examine them. While they were doing that a dark, trousered figure appeared in a clearing about a hundred yards away and Ellen Grae, who didn't have any interest in the tracks, sucked her breath in and said, "Oh, glory, look!"

"Ellen Grae," Grover said. "It's just a man. These are the funniest-looking tracks I ever saw. I wonder what kind they are."

Ellen Grae ran over and squatted between the two boys. Her breath on Grover's face was hot. She seized his arm. In each of her eyes there appeared a large, black exclamation mark. "Grover, you know who that is standing out there looking at us?"

"He's not looking at us, Ellen Grae. What—"

"That's Monk Ford!"

"Who's Monk Ford?"

"From the post office! From the post office!"

"Well, maybe he's got the day off. What're you so excited about?"

Ellen Grae's smile was bloodless. Her lips moved rigidly up and down against her teeth with each jerk of her breath. "Grover, I don't mean that's Monk Ford who *works* in the post office! I mean that's Monk Ford whose *picture* is in the post office! He's a fugitive from Tennessee justice! Oh, glory! I suppose it's our duty to try and apprehend him!"

Grover looked around again at Monk Ford. Monk was standing there in the clearing just looking up at some trees like he was debating whether to climb them or not. For some reason he didn't look like any fugitive from justice. For some reason he didn't look a bit unfriendly. There was something in his loose stance and careless slouch of hat that just wouldn't let crime come to mind.

Grover said, "Ellen Grae, I don't think we ought to do anything. I don't think that's Monk Ford. Of course, I can't see his face too well from this distance and I don't see how you can either but I don't think that's any criminal. He just doesn't look like one. He looks too . . . round."

Ellen Grae wouldn't listen to him. She said he wasn't a good citizen. She said that he could shirk his citizen's duty if he wanted to but that she was going to follow Monk Ford and find out what he was up to—find out where his hiding place was. And then she was going to go back to town and get Sheriff Fudge. Probably Sheriff Fudge would call in the FBI since Monk's crime, stealing postal money orders when the clerk wasn't looking, involved the Federal Government.

While Ellen Grae was telling Farrell and Grover all of this they forgot to keep an eye on Monk and he disappeared. It was as if the earth had just quietly opened up and swallowed him. One minute he was standing there with the luminous rays of the sun on him, looking up in the trees, and the next he was gone.

Ellen Grae declared that this was Grover's fault. "If I didn't have to explain everything to you and Farrell all the time it wouldn't have happened," she declared with a wild, thwarted look. "I swear, Grover, sometimes you aggravate the heck out of me."

Farrell said, "Now, lambie, you shouldn't talk to Grover like that."

Grover said, "Ellen Grae, probably it's for the best. Come on, let's go back to the boat. It's time to eat."

Ellen Grae thrust out her lower, martyred lip. "No, Grover. You and Farrell go on back to the boat and wait for me there if you want to, but it's my citizen's duty to find out where Monk Ford's hiding place is out here and I'm going to perform it."

In the end they were obliged to go with her. The swamp was no place for a lone girl—not even Ellen Grae.

They stalked Monk for two torrid, sweaty, exhaustive hours. Grover never spotted him but Ellen Grae and Farrell did. Monk was everywhere—crouched behind a downed tree, sitting motionless in a stand of high, weaving grass, lying in a murky slough, his face draped in a swirl of Spanish moss for camouflage. Once he beckoned to them from a distant rise in the land and once they heard his sinister laugh very close but they didn't catch him or find out where his hiding place was. They wound up back at the spot they had started from.

"I know this is where we started from because I forgot my hat," said Ellen Grae retrieving it and setting it on her sweat-drenched head. "Lordy. I don't know about you two but I'm tuckered. Whew."

Grover was tuckered, too, and parched-thirsty. There was a trembling weakness in his arms and a drumming in his chest. To catch his breath he sat down.

Farrell laid down. He said he didn't care if an alligator came up and bit him—that he was so tired he wouldn't be able to lift a finger to help himself if it did.

Ellen Grae limped over and propped herself against the tree that overshadowed them and gave attention to her mosquito bites and scratches but after a second she stopped scratching and rubbing and the queerest expression came over her face.

Grover said, "Ellen Grae, what now?"

She said, "Grover, we're being watched. Do you feel eyes on you?"

"No, Ellen Grae. I don't feel a thing except thirst."

"I feel eyes on me," said Ellen Grae and tilted her head and looked up in the branches of the tree. Farrell and Grover let their eyes follow hers and they saw a strange sight. Mrs. Merriweather, on leave from her plant nursery, was up there sitting straddle-legged in a two-pronged fork. A camera dangled from a strap which was wrapped around her neck. She was absorbed in the study of two air plants which had attached themselves to the tree's bark and grown to monstrous sizes. Her slouch hat hung from a nearby peg. She had a notebook propped open on one trousered knee and was writing in it as she studied.

In a loud, vibrant voice Ellen Grae said, "Well, you'd think after all the trouble she put us to she'd at least speak to us."

Farrell said, "Now, lambie, she didn't ask us to chase her when she wasn't running. We just did it."

Grover said, "Ellen Grae, she probably isn't wearing her hearing aid. She doesn't look like she is and she's deaf as a doornail without it. She doesn't even know we're here."

Ellen Grae's face was as red as a beet but after a minute she laughed and Farrell and Grover did, too.

On the way home Farrell caught three good-sized catfish. They took them home to Rose and she made a stew out of them.

Farrell and Ellen Grae went home and got cleaned up and came back to eat supper. Farrell said he was hungry as a bear but when Rose set his bowl of stew before him he changed his mind after one look. He said, "Oh, my gosh. Oh, my gosh." And turned green, even to the tips of his ears.

Grover's father said, "What's the matter?"

"There's a head in it," whispered Farrell. "It shouldn't be there, should it?"

Grover's father's smile was slow and faint. Still, it *was* a smile—the first Grover had seen on his father's face since his mother left. He had Rose take the fish head out of Farrell's bowl and put it in his own. Farrell wouldn't eat any of the stew though, even without the head in it. Rose had to make him two peanut butter and jelly sandwiches.